Blue's Adventures

To Kain

Best wishes

Maggie Jones

xxx

Maggie Jones

Printed in the United Kingdom

First Printing, 2014 Alfie Dog Limited

The author can be found at: authors@alfiedog.com

With thanks to Anna Cusick, Westmead Teddies, Godshill, IOW, for the use of Blue for the cover photograph.

ISBN 978-1-909894-24-2

Published by
Alfie Dog Limited
Schilde Lodge, Tholthorpe,
North Yorkshire, YO61 1SN
Tel: 0207 193 33 90

DEDICATION

For Lauren, Christy & Nathan with all my love

CONTENTS

ACKNOWLEDGMENTS

With sincere thanks to my publisher Rosemary J. Kind, without whose continued encouragement with my writing, I would not be where I am today.

I would very much like to say what a privilege it was for me to write about, the Isle of Wight, but especially the pretty little village of Godshill where I live. Many thanks also go to Deliwe, Eden & Liam Mwamuka for their contributions for my stories Blue's Show and Tell Adventure, and Blue's Football Adventure, without all your support, I would never have been able to tell my stories so well.

Lastly, I want to thank my work colleagues and friends from The Wight Fair Writers for their backing and praise when I thought I was getting nowhere with my stories. However, I think the person who so deserves my heartfelt gratitude is my husband Graeme, who has cooked, cleaned and looked after the family, whilst I have been busy writing, editing, re-editing. I could not have done it without your fantastic support.

1
BLUE'S CHRISTMAS EVE ADVENTURE

Christmas Eve at the toy shop had been a very busy one. Right up until the last minute mums and dads had been rushing in to buy their children the must have new toy on the market. Some fighting over the last few remaining ones, until at the end of the day, all that was left on the shelf was the tattiest blue teddy bear anyone had ever seen.

Blue had unfortunately had his day. Many years ago bears like him had been the most popular toy in the shops, but not now. Since then he'd seen other new toys come and go, but sadly not him. All he'd ever wanted was to be bought so he could be loved by someone and have adventures with his new owner, but that hadn't happened. And here he was stuck once again, as the last toy left on the shelf.

He pulled himself up from his sitting position and wandered gingerly along towards the end of the shelf. He wasn't as young as he used to be and his joints were a little stiff. The Christmas tree was on the counter; the lights twinkling brightly as he gently clambered on to the top branches climbing slowly down. He looked around him when he reached the safety of the counter.

Sighing heavily, he rubbed his eyes as he looked back at the now empty shelf. It wasn't fair, no one seemed to want him, they didn't want a blue teddy bear when there was a red fire engine, or a super space toy that was all the rage now instead.

Suddenly he heard something. Was it a jingling noise? No it couldn't have been it must have been his imagination. Then he heard the sound of heavy footsteps making their way down… the chimney! The next things he saw were big black boots with the top of stocking legs. Blue rubbed his eyes again, not believing what he was actually seeing as the boots moved forwards and a large man in a red suit with a long white beard bent down and emerged from under the chimney breast. He gently pulled himself upright chuckling away.

Blue, as quickly as he could, ran and hid behind the Christmas tree. He was frightened. No one was supposed to know that toys came alive when there wasn't anyone around. If he'd had a heart, he was sure it would have been beating furiously as he desperately tried to keep still and out of sight. However, he was intrigued by this mysterious man with the deep chuckle.

He gingerly poked his head out from behind the tree, wondering what the man was doing. Blue watched in amazement as he saw him pulling a great big red sack out from behind him.

'Now then where's that list I had?'

Blue heard the man talking to himself. List what list? He was curious and edged himself out even further from behind the tree as he began to wonder what on earth was inside the huge sack too.

'If I don't find that list, my wife, Mrs Christmas is going to be extremely cross with me. We had everything we needed at Lapland, but not that one thing, which for the life of me I can't remember what it was now!' The man was talking to himself, scratching his head over his red hat and every time he moved, the little bell at the top of it would jingle.

Blue was certainly intrigued and listened carefully, trying to work out for himself just what it was this Mr Christmas wanted in a toy store, which no longer had any more toys in it, apart from him! And Blue didn't think Mr Christmas would want him. He looked sadly at his reflection in one of the shiny baubles hanging on the tree beside him.

Once where his fur had been the brightest blue, it had now paled considerably. That was due to sitting for so long on the shelf in the bright lights and with the sun shining in through the window over the years. Also his stitching was starting to come undone. He'd tried hard not to pick at it, but it hadn't been easy. What had started out as one little thread had niggled, until he'd pulled most of the seam apart.

He was intently looking at where the hole was on his chest, so he didn't see Mr Christmas approach him.

'Well, what do we have here then?' Mr Christmas said as he picked up Blue and looked at him noticing his hole too, as he put his finger in it. That tickled Blue and he laughed out loud, but suddenly he stopped.

'Oh you do talk, that's splendid, little chap,' Mr Christmas said ruffling Blue behind his ears making him giggle again.

'You have got an infectious little giggle haven't you?' Mr Christmas said suddenly laughing out loud himself, although his laugh was more of a 'ho ho ho'.

'Now little blue bear do you think you could do me a favour?'

At that Blue, although still slightly wary of this jolly large man, nodded.

'What I need is someone small like you to climb into

my big red sack and see if you can find the list Mrs Christmas gave me. I can't seem to find it anywhere. Do you think you can do that for me?' He asked.

Blue looked cautiously at Mr Christmas before nodding again.

'The list could be anywhere. And as you are so small, you are just the right size to look into all the nooks and crannies in this sack. Now I know you're probably thinking, why not just empty it all out, but if I did that, I would never get them all put back in time, and make it to all the places I need to get to by the end of tonight. And that can never happen; I have never disappointed any child ever by not getting to them with their presents before morning,' Mr Christmas said sternly.

Blue suddenly felt terribly excited. He felt as if he were on some sort of adventure, which was silly really, as all he was being asked to do was go into a sack and look for a list!

Gently Mr Christmas picked Blue up and placed him on top of the sack.

'Off you go.'

As soon as he was placed in it, he started to feel his way around. He couldn't see the list, or feel it as the sack started getting darker the nearer the bottom he got. Suddenly he felt the sack move, as he was pushed up against a large wrapped gift; it was almost as if the sack were being lifted up, but that couldn't be right. He looked up towards the top of the sack, there was no light, the cord on it had been done up tightly.

'Help, help, let me out.' Blue shouted as hard as he could, but knew he couldn't be heard above the jingling of the bells he could hear in the background. In the end he decided to make himself as comfortable as possible. He supposed now he really was having an adventure.

Suddenly the cord was pulled back and a hand came into the bag and grabbed hold of a couple of gifts. Blue tried to get Mr Christmas's attention.

'Hello, I'm still here?'

But obviously Mr Christmas hadn't heard him, because as soon as the gifts had been removed, the cord was tied back up again and that continued to happen until there weren't any more gifts left and Blue was the only toy left in the sack. He realised now that as the bag got emptied, there was no list in there either. Mr Christmas must have had it on him all the time!

He started to wonder how long it would be before Mr Christmas remembered he was in the sack. He didn't have long to wait, as before no time the cord was being pulled open again and a hand was coming into the bag and gently taking hold of him.

'Well thank goodness you're still here, because you are just what I need.' Mr Christmas beamed as he looked at him.

Blue looked stunned!

Suddenly there was a blinding light and Blue had to squeeze his eyes tightly shut. When he opened them he couldn't believe it as he looked down at himself. Where the hole had been it was gone, now it was neatly sewn up. Even looking at his fur it somehow seemed brighter. And the finishing touch was the big red bow that was tied neatly around his little neck.

He looked around him and saw that they were in a dimly lit room with lots of beds in it. There were children lying fast asleep in them.

'Little blue bear you're adventure with me is now over. You are at the end of it, but hopefully you'll have lots more adventures with Jack Foster. You see he's been poorly, but he's on the mend now. He has always wanted a teddy bear as a gift and Mrs Christmas and I decided that it was high time you were that someone special's gift.'

Blue couldn't believe his ears as he was gently placed onto the end of the bed. He was the first thing Jack saw when he woke up just a few hours later. His shrieks of delight made Blue feel so happy, especially when Jack put his arms around him and hugged him close to his small body.

'Oh wow, a teddy bear. My very own teddy bear, I shall call you Blue bear, and we shall have lots of adventures when I come out of hospital. What do you say to that Blue?'

Blue just looked at Jack and smiled. After all this time, he was finally going to be loved by someone. And most of all it seemed this was the start of all the adventures he felt sure he was going to have from now on with Jack.

2
BLUE'S SNOW TIME ADVENTURE

It was early Christmas morning when Blue saw the look of excitement on Jack's face, as Jack took in just who was sitting on the end of his bed. It had really made his day; Jack couldn't believe he had actually got a teddy bear! And, Blue, couldn't believe that after spending years in the toy shop, now he was going to be part of Jack's family and hopefully have adventures galore.

When Jack had been discharged from hospital, even the journey home had, in Blue's eyes, been an adventure as he'd sat in the back of Jack's dad's 4 x 4, being held closely in Jack's arms. Blue enjoyed looking out of the window as they drove through Newport, seeing the Christmas lights and decorations in the High Street and all the shops, before eventually leaving the town. And then all he saw was the passing scenery of fields and countryside.

Then just a short while later; they were pulling into a driveway.

'We're home, Blue,' Jack said excitedly as he very slowly inched his way out of the back seat.

It had been difficult for Jack to get around as the break in his left leg had been a bad one. Manoeuvring his way out of the car, with Blue still clasped tightly in his arms, and trying to get into the wheel chair, the hospital had lent them, was quite a feat, but somehow he managed it.

Whilst at the hospital, the nurses decided that to make Jack feel better, they would put a plaster cast on Blue's left leg too! He was glad he was being carried and didn't have to struggle into his own wheel chair.

Blue wondered what was happening to him when one of the nurses had suddenly whisked him off to a side room. She'd carefully placed him down on a table.

'Now then, we don't want to ruin your fur, so if I put this plastic bag over your left leg, then it should protect it,' the nurse said to him as she wound a cast on top of it.

It felt a little awkward at first, but then Blue, like Jack got used to it.

Jack lived with Tom his older brother, and his parents, Matthew and Elizabeth, in a chalet bungalow in Godshill on the Isle of Wight. Jack had his own room, and luckily for him; it was on the ground floor, next door to his brother's room.

When Jack took Blue inside for the first time, Blue looked around the room and liked what he saw. Jack had a bed that looked like an aeroplane. On one wall of his room the wallpaper matched the duvet cover, which was covered in planes too.

Jack also had other toys in his room, but Blue needn't have worried if they would be friendly or not, as when Jack fell asleep they made Blue feel very welcome. They were so pleased that Jack had at long last got his wish for a teddy bear.

During the rest of the school holidays, Blue, Jack and the other toys played as much as they could, until it was time for Jack and Tom to return to school.

Jack was told he would still be able to go, as he could use the wheelchair to be pushed around in. And, it was made all the easier for him as he took Blue with him to keep him company.

Blue loved all the fuss he received, especially when

everyone laughed when they noticed the similarity between the two of them, with their left legs in plaster!

'Wow, what a wonderful teddy bear,' Molly Bucket, the girl who sat next to Jack in the classroom said.

For a while, Blue and Jack were the centre of attention. All Jack's school friends wanted to hold Blue, whilst stroking his bright blue fur.

However, soon the day came when they had to go back to the hospital to have their casts removed. When they came out of school on Friday afternoon, Mum was waiting for them, to take them and also to return the wheelchair.

Blue was slightly disappointed, as he'd had so much fun with Jack's friends, especially as they took it in turns in pushing them both around in the wheelchair.

And if the truth be known, he was a little afraid that having the cast cut from his leg would hurt.

But, he needn't have worried, as the nurse took care with both him and Jack. And the good thing was she asked Jack if he would like to keep the casts.

'Oh yes please, because all my friends have signed both of them,' Jack said smiling at her as she wrapped them up in a plastic bag, before handing them over to him.

On the drive home Mum looked up at the sky.

'That sky looks threatening,' she said.

'What do you mean, Mum?' Jack said cuddling Blue.

'The weather forecasters said we might have snow, and looking at that sky, it wouldn't surprise me if they were right. It certainly is cold enough,' she said shivering.

Back home it was nice and warm; Dad had got the wood burner going.

'I bet that feels better not having that cast on any longer?' he said looking at Jack and Blue.

'It does, doesn't it pal?' Jack said turning to Blue. 'Dad, Mum says we might have snow. Do you think we will?'

'Well the weatherman's just been on saying that there is a possibility in the South East, so we'll have to wait and see. Sometimes, we tend to miss out, because of the stretch of water between us and the mainland. So don't get your hopes up.'

Jack nodded looking disappointed.

'Right then, let's have some tea, and then I can bath you, before bed,' Mum said. 'You never know when you wake up in the morning it might have snowed.'

When Jack went to bed that night he turned to Blue and said, 'Let's pray for snow, Blue.'

The following morning, it looked as if Jack's prayers had been answered especially when Jack got up out of bed and pulled the curtain back. Grabbing hold of Blue, he rushed into his brother's bedroom, shouting at him.

'Tom, Tom wake up, look it's snowed,' he said, before hurrying to the window and pulling back Tom's curtains, as he looked out.

He turned back to Tom with the biggest smile on his face.

'Do you think Dad will let us get the sledge out and take it to the park to go sledging?' Jack asked as he threw Blue in the air, catching him in his arms and hugging him.

'Are you ready for another adventure, pal?' he asked Blue, as he hugged him close to his chest. 'You and me are going sledging, what do you think about that?'

Blue wasn't too sure. He'd never been out in snow before, let alone gone sledging in it. Whatever sledging was.

Sitting on the top shelf of the toy store over the years, he had seen the white stuff as it fell from the sky covering everything in sight. He had also seen people outside slipping and falling in it too. He was a little afraid; would he have a good snow time?

However, before he could think about it anymore, he heard Mum calling them.

'Boys, time for breakfast.'

'We're just coming, Mum,' they shouted back.

They raced to get dressed and into the kitchen to eat their breakfast as quickly as they could.

'That's got to be a first from you two,' Dad said looking at Mum and smiling, 'getting up so quickly, especially on a Saturday. It can't have anything to do with the snow outside, can it?'

'Mum, Dad, can we go out and play in it after breakfast?' Tom asked as he sat there gulping his cereal down. 'Not so fast, Tom, you'll choke.' She chided him, as he nodded quickly.

'Yes, we can all go outside. How about I go out into the shed and see if I can find the sledge that we bought last year and didn't get the chance to use?' Dad said. The boys bobbed their heads up and down enthusiastically.

Dad downed his coffee before going and putting on his coat and wellies. Both boys finished their breakfast in record time and rushed to clean their teeth.

Afterwards as Jack and Tom pulled on their coats, and wellies, Mum came out into the hallway holding scarves, gloves and hats in her hands.

'Here you go, don't forget to put these on too. They'll keep you warm,' she said.

'Thanks, Mum,' both boys chorused back.

'Jack, here I had some wool left over and made a small scarf and hat for Blue,' she said holding out an identical pair for him.

'Thanks, Mum.' Jack beamed at her as he raced to fetch Blue, who he'd left behind in the kitchen, sitting on the breakfast bar.

Quickly untying the blue ribbon from around Blue's neck, Jack replaced it with the scarf. He had to struggle slightly with the hat, pulling it determinedly down on top of Blue's head and making sure it stayed in place with a firm tug. And then they were finally ready for their adventure in the snow.

Dad took the boys to the local play park. They dragged the sledge behind them and then Dad told Jack to wait while he and Tom pulled it up the slight hill.

'You're going to enjoy riding on the sledge,' Jack said to Blue.

Although, Blue wasn't too sure as they watched Dad and Tom ride back down to the bottom again. Then it was their go, as Dad told Tom to wait while he went back again with Jack.

'Are you ready, Blue?' Jack asked him. They both clung on tightly as they started their trip back down.

'Yippee, this is good fun, isn't it, Blue?' Jack shouted out.

Blue had to agree, as he loved every minute of it. The thrilling and exhilarating ride down the hill was over in mere minutes. Smiling broadly at his dad, Jack squeezed Blue tightly when they joined Tom at the bottom again.

'Right one more go for you both, and then we can have a snow ball fight,' Dad said as he and Tom started walking up the hill again.

'Come on, Blue; help me make the best snowballs ever,' Jack said placing Blue down onto the ground as he grabbed a load of snow and started scrunching it into balls. He was determined he was going to win that fight at any cost.

Unfortunately, because Jack was so busy collecting snow, he didn't see his dad and brother coming down the hill at an alarmingly fast rate, but Blue did.

Blue cried out, 'Jack!'

Jack could have sworn he heard someone calling his name and he only turned at the last minute. When he did, he saw that Dad and Tom were heading straight for…Blue.

'Blue!' Jack shouted out as he rushed over to save his little friend from being swept away.

Luckily for Blue, Jack got to him just in time, although, he didn't get out of the way of the speeding sledge, and was knocked down by it.

'Ow, my leg it really hurts,' Jack sobbed, as Dad rushed over to him and hugged him close to his chest. It was clear that something was wrong as Jack started crying and yowling in pain.

'It looks like it might be another trip to casualty,' Dad said grimacing at Jack's sad face.

At casualty it was revealed that Jack had this time broken his… right leg. And Blue knew what that meant!

The look of shock on Jack's school friends faces on Monday morning was really funny to see, as they all rushed over to sign both casts again and also to wheel Jack and Blue around in the wheel chair once more.

3
BLUE'S VALENTINE ADVENTURE

One Monday morning, Blue was happily sitting in the back of Jack's rucksack. They were getting ready to go to school. On the walk to the local primary school Blue could see lots of exciting things, like different flowers that had just come into bud and the village starting to come to life after the winter. However, when they got to Westmead Teddies shop Blue had a shock!

'I love this shop,' Mum said stopping and gazing in the window. 'It's great having a shop in the village that sells teddy bears of all shapes and sizes.'

Jack nodded, 'Me too!'

'Oh, look, Anna's done a new display?' Mum said. 'What a beautiful pink teddy bear.'

'That means they will be opening again soon,' Jack said smiling happily. 'I'll be able to show Anna my Blue bear. I bet she won't ever have seen a bear like my Blue before.'

'Mum, why do they close after Christmas?' Tom asked.

'It's so the teddies and Anna and Andy, can have a well-deserved rest,' Mum said winking at Jack and Blue.

'Come on boys, we'd best get going,' Mum said urging them on.

Just as they walked past the window, Blue couldn't believe it when the pink teddy bear, which Mum liked, winked and smiled at him. He rubbed his eyes, was he seeing things? He shook his head. Jack was walking very quickly, trying to catch up with his mum and brother, so Blue convinced himself that he'd imagined it.

School was fun, and once again the day flew past. Before long, Mum was standing at the gates waiting to take Jack and Tom home again. As they walked along the road, they stopped once again at Westmead Teddies.

'I really do love this display that Anna's done. It is so pretty with all the hearts and red bows around the window. And look at that really cute pink teddy bear.' Mum said, tapping her finger on the window, pointing out the bear to the boys.

'She is a pretty little bear, but, why has she got hearts on her dress and a red bow on the top of her head?' Jack said scrunching his face up towards the window.

'It's because she's for Valentine's Day, which is just a couple of weeks away,' Mum said smiling at him.

'Valentine's Day, what's that?' Jack asked.

'Well, it actually used to be called Saint Valentine's Day, or the Feast of Saint Valentine and is celebrated on the14th of February, every year. Ladies and gentlemen, boys and girls, show how much they love one another by giving flowers, chocolates and other gifts on that day. Usually, cards are sent, and you're not supposed to sign the card so the person receiving it doesn't know who sent it. It's a bit like having a secret admirer.' Mum laughed.

'Do you and Dad send cards and have gifts?' Jack asked, completely fascinated.

'Well, sometimes we get each other a little gift, but not always. Your dad knows just how much I love him, and vice versa. And, it's not always about having a gift, although that's nice too.' She laughed again.

'Are you getting him a present and card this year?'

'Well, I expect so, although I haven't given it much thought.'

'Do you think Dad will get you something?' Jack

asked, as Mum turned and looked in the shop window again.

'I don't know, but it would be nice. By the way, did you also know, that when we have a Leap Year, on the 29th February, it's traditional that ladies can propose to men and ask them to marry them?'

'Did you do that to Dad?' Tom asked.

Mum's face went bright red, as she shyly nodded.

'I did.'

'Did he say yes?' Jack asked.

Mum burst out laughing, before saying, 'Yes, silly.'

Tom looked at Jack and started laughing too.

'Stop laughing at me, Tom. If you know so much, did you know what Valentine's Day is?'

'Yes, of course I do.' Tom said smugly.

'Why, have you got a girlfriend?' Jack asked, watching as Tom's face went a vivid shade of red.

'Tom's got a girlfriend, Tom's got a girlfriend,' Jack called out skipping along the road.

'Jack, stop saying that,' Tom said.

'Oh, you're going to kiss a girl. Yuck!' Jack said, watching Tom's face go an even deeper shade of red.

'Mum, tell Jack to stop.' Tom was getting angry.

'Jack, that's enough. Don't be mean to your brother,' Mum said, but she was smiling.

'Sorry,' Jack said looking at Tom, before giggling and hugging Blue. 'Shall I give you a big kiss, Blue?' he said laughing at his pal.

'Mum…' Tom said looking at Jack, as she raised her eyes.

Jack bent his head, giggling into Blue's fur.

'You're not funny, Jack.' Tom said as he pushed past him.

Jack giggled away, still hugging Blue.

Every day they walked past the teddy bear shop and Mum would stop and look in the window, gazing at the pink teddy. And every day, Blue would see the same teddy, smile and wink at him, when no one else was looking.

He started winking back at her too, and waving his paw, when Jack wasn't looking. Blue thought, there had to be a way of getting to meet her properly.

One day when they were walking home from school, and Mum had stopped at the window, Blue looked at the door to the shop and saw the sign was turned around.

It was open for business!

'Oh, hang on, boys,' Mum said calling them back as they'd already walked past the shop. 'Anna's got the shop open, and I want to go in and ask about something.'

'And, I can show her my Blue bear,' Jack said feeling excited, taking his rucksack off his shoulders and pulling Blue out of it.

The bell on the door rang as they walked in and Anna came out from the back.

'Hello, how lovely to see you,' Anna said smiling at them. 'Are you all well?'

'We're really well, thanks Anna…'

Before Mum could say another word Jack butted in, pushing Blue forward.

'Do you like my Blue bear? When I woke up in hospital on Christmas morning, he was sitting on the end of my bed,' he said.

'He's lovely, and very old. If I didn't know any better I would say he looked like a Michtom bear, except they are so old and extremely rare so he probably isn't.' Anna stroked his fur gently, 'I expect you look after him very well?' she said looking closely at Blue, before putting him down onto the counter.

Jack nodded. 'He goes everywhere with me.'

'Why don't you all come into the back and I'll put the kettle on and you can tell me how Jack ended up in hospital?' Anna said to Mum.

'Are you sure? I thought you were open for business.'

'No, I was just testing the water today, and I've had a couple of sales, but I know the coaches, that go to the Old Smithy up the road, will have all gone back to their hotels now,' she said as Mum nodded. 'Tom, can you turn the sign round on the door, and pull the catch down on it for me, please?' Anna asked.

Tom did as he was asked and followed Mum, Jack and Anna into the back to the kitchen. The lights went out in the shop, and Blue was left on the counter. He looked to the front of the shop where the pink teddy bear was. He thought she was the most beautiful teddy bear he'd ever seen, and would have given anything to speak to her. But he was scared!

Suddenly, the pink teddy bear looked directly at him and waved.

'Hello there, my name's Rose. Did I hear that little boy call you… Blue?'

Blue nodded, lost for words. Rose was carefully making her way towards him. She climbed out of the front window gently clambering down to the floor.

'Can you get down from there, using those?' Rose said to Blue indicating some cardboard boxes that were next to the counter.

Blue nodded, and moved over to the boxes, making his way down to the floor by holding on to the edge of each box until he was standing in front of Rose.

'What type of bear are you?' Rose asked Blue.

'I am a very old type of bear, although I don't remember what type,' he said smiling at her. 'What type of bear are you?'

'I am a special edition bear, made especially for Valentine's Day,' she said proudly twirling around for Blue.

'You are very pretty,' Blue said quietly.

'Thank you and you are a handsome bear too.' She giggled.

'I like waving at you, but this is much nicer to be able to talk to you,' Blue said shyly.

Rose giggled and nodded.

'Have you been with your owner very long?' Rose asked

'Since Christmas Day,' Blue said, going on to tell Rose all about his adventure with Mr Christmas.

'Oh, I really hope that someone buys me soon, so that I can have adventures with my new owner. You are so lucky,' Rose said smiling at Blue.

Blue nodded.

'I think I had better get back into the window, before Anna comes out again. Will you still wave to me every day?'

'Yes, of course I will.'

And, Blue hoped that he would be able to wave to her for a very long time to come, as Rose made her way over to the window. However, before she could climb back up, and Blue could get back onto the counter, the lights went on in the shop.

'I can't believe you broke both your legs in such a short space of time. You were very lucky; that the second break wasn't as bad as the first, and you're leg wasn't in plaster for too long,' Anna said to Jack as they came back into the shop.

'Blue!' Jack shouted out when he saw his pal lying on the floor. 'What are you doing down there?' He picked him up and dusted him off before cuddling him close.

'What's going on here?' Anna said, walking forward into the shop where she went over to Rose lying on the floor too, picking her up and dusting her down, before placing her back into the window.

'I reckon that teddy bear came over to say hello to my Blue bear,' Jack said, as Mum and Anna exchanged smiles.

'You do, do you? Well this is one very special teddy bear. Her name is Rose, and she has been commissioned especially for Valentine's Day. When she was designed, her creators also designed several outfits for her too. So anyone who buys her can also buy them, if they want to change her clothes for different occasions.'

'She really is a lovely bear,' Mum said touching Rose's soft fur.

'Well whoever buys her will have to have lots of money. She is one very expensive teddy bear.'

'Oh,' Mum said sadly.

Blue looked at Mum's face. Why was she sad?

When they got home, Dad was there, he'd already started making the tea.

'Is ham, egg and chips alright for tea?' He asked as they walked in through the door.

'That's smashing, Dad, it's my favourite,' Jack said.

'Well go and wash your hands you two boys, while Mum and I set the table.'

The boys nodded and left Mum and Dad to get the cutlery out. Blue heard Dad ask where they'd been, and Mum explained that they had stopped at the teddy bear shop.

'They have the most adorable pink bear in the window. Her name is Rose and she is a special edition bear for Valentine's Day. But she's really expensive,' Mum said shaking her head.

Dad gave her a quizzical glance.

'You like the teddy bear?'

Mum nodded.

'I do. It's silly really, but that bear, she reminded me of the teddy bear I had when I was a little girl. My bear was called Emily. I named her after my best friend Emily Bradley. Emily and I grew up together, but she and her family emigrated to Australia and as a parting gift to her, I gave her my Emily. This bear reminded me of Emily and she brought back lots of memories.'

'You've never mentioned Emily before,' Dad said.

'I know, because we lost touch with one another. We always meant to keep in contact. And although, I did have her address, when I moved out from home I lost a lot of my paperwork, including my address book. And when I asked my Mum if she could remember Emily's parents address, she couldn't,' she said unhappily.

Blue listened and thought it was sad.

Just then the boys came back into the kitchen.

'They're all clean,' Jack said showing his parents his hands.

'That's good then. Go and sit down and I'll dish up,' Dad said smiling at him.

Over the next few days, every time they walked past the shop on the way to and from school, Mum would stop and stare at Rose, and Blue would smile and wave to her when no one else was looking. Rose would always wave back to him too.

And then, the day before Valentine's Day, when they were walking past Westmead Teddies Mum did a double take.

'Can you hang on, boys?' she asked walking back to the window.

'Why, Mum?' Jack said coming to stand beside her.

Blue, who for a change was being cuddled by Jack, could immediately see what the problem was. Rose wasn't in the front window. He could see Mum peering in through the door.

'Oh, it's nothing. It's just that pink teddy bear isn't in the window; I just wondered if Anna had moved her,' she said.

'Perhaps Anna sold her,' Jack said. 'If she did, the teddy bear must have gone to a special home, because she was a lot of money, wasn't she?'

Mum sadly nodded.

'Yes, she was a very expensive bear. Come along, we'd better get you boys to school, then I've got to get to work at the doctors,' she said gloomily.

Blue was devastated. No longer would he see Rose in the window and smile and wave to her! He looked at Mum's face and knew exactly how she felt. Even being with Jack at school, did nothing to cheer him up.

On the walk home from school, Blue hoped that Mum would go and see Anna, and ask her what had happened to Rose. Unfortunately, when Jack and Tom came out of school, it wasn't Mum who was standing there waiting for them, but Dad, and he'd come in his old 4 x 4.

'Hello, boys, Mum's had to stay at work today, she's covering for someone who's off sick.'

Blue was so disappointed. Would he ever find out what had happened to Rose?

By the time Mum came home from work, the boys were bathed and ready for bed. Dad was reading them both a bedtime story as Mum came in to kiss them goodnight. They were in Jack's room for the story.

'I've just come to say goodnight,' she said bending down to kiss Jack on the cheek, before going over to Tom to do the same to him.

'Are you okay?' Dad asked Mum.

She nodded her head. 'I'm just tired that's all. I think I'll go and have a nice bath,' she said smiling at them before she went out of the room.

'It's Valentine's Day tomorrow, have you got Mum a card and a present?' Jack asked his Dad.

Dad's face paled.

'Did you say it was Valentine's Day, tomorrow?'

Jack looked at Tom.

'Dad, you haven't forgotten, have you?' Tom said, before Jack butted in. 'Mum, will be so upset.'

'Don't worry boys, I'm onto it.' He laughed. 'Look, I think we'd better finish the story for now. I've got something to do,' he said standing up and kissing Jack before tucking him and Blue up in bed. Shooing Tom out of the door and to his bedroom, Dad followed behind him.

Jack heard Dad shout out to Mum, 'I'm going out for a while. See you later.'

'Oh dear, Blue, I really hope Dad gets Mum something.'

Blue was thinking the same thing.

The next day dawned bright and sunny, and this year Valentine's Day was a Saturday. Jack heard the letter box go as the postman delivered some letters.

'Let's go and see what the postman has brought, Blue,' Jack said swinging his legs out of bed as he raced to the

23

hall, clutching his pal.

There were two brown letters that were addressed to Mum and Dad, but there was also a surprise. There were cards for him, Tom and Mum!

Walking into the kitchen with the letters and card in his hands Jack took them over to Mum who was sitting at the table.

'Here you go, Mum,' he said handing them over to her.

Mum had been looking a bit glum, but she instantly brightened up when she saw the card in Jack's hand.

'Me and Tom have got cards too!' Jack said giving Tom his card.

Tom's face went a vivid shade of red as he took the card from Jack.

'Aren't you going to open it?' Jack said looking at Tom, as he tore open his card.

"Happy Valentine's Day" it read on the front. Jack opened the card to see who it was from. But, all it said on the inside was, "To Jack, from your valentine."

His face said it all. 'Who would send me a Valentine's card? I don't know any girls, yuck, and if I did. I wouldn't send them a Valentine's card.'

Mum laughed as Jack screwed up his face.

'Of course you know girls, what about Molly and Charlotte from your school?'

'Do you think one of them sent me this card?' Jack asked incredulously.

Mum just shrugged her shoulders at him.

Suddenly, Tom smiled and opened his card. It said exactly the same thing on his card as Jack's did.

'They're from you,' he said pointing his finger at his mum and bursting out laughing as he too looked at Jack's face.

Jack felt relieved.

Mum nodded and giggled. 'I thought it would be nice for you two to receive your first Valentine's cards.'

'Are you going to open your card?' Jack said looking at the card Mum still had in her hand.

She nodded and tore the envelope open, pulling the card out from it.

"To my Valentine" it read on the front.

Mum opened the card and smiled.

'Well who's it from?' Jack asked eagerly.

'It's from my Valentine,' Mum said, turning the card round to show him.

At that moment, Dad walked into the kitchen. In his hands he held a big bouquet of roses.

'Happy Valentine's Day,' he said going up to Mum and giving her a kiss.

'Yuck!' Jack said grimacing at them.

'The same to you, and here's a card for you,' Mum said smiling at Dad as he tore it open. Inside was a voucher.

'Thanks, that's great, just what I wanted,' Dad said smiling at her. 'By the way, I hope you haven't made plans for tonight, Madam,' Dad said putting on a posh voice.

Mum shook her head.

'That's good, because tonight I will be creating a culinary delight for you. Yes, last night I created a wonderful meal of ham, egg and chips, and tonight I am going to create an even greater meal for you. I shall be cooking, drum roll, please... beans on toast!'

At that, Mum and the boys laughed out loud.

'No, really, I'm giving beans on toast to the boys, and they will be having an early night,' he said looking at them, 'and then I want to amaze you for your tea. I am going to cook something that will make you gasp in surprise. Will that be alright?' Dad asked.

'I can't wait. Now I'd better get these roses into some water. They are really beautiful,' Mum said smelling them.

The day went by very quickly, and before too long the boys were having their baked beans on toast for tea. As soon as they'd finished, Mum whisked them away for a bath, whilst Dad laid the table for their meal.

'Something smells nice, Dad,' Jack said when he and Tom came to say goodnight.

'Why thank you very much. I've made Mum a dish that Nannie told me your Mum likes. It's called Boeuf Bourguignon.'

The boys nodded, before Jack spotted something.

'Dad, why have you set another place at the table? I thought Valentine's Day was supposed to be for two people.'

'Ah ha, you will have to wait until tomorrow to find out. Now off to bed with you both. And I don't want to hear a peep from you.'

'Yes, Dad,' they said going towards their bedrooms, grinning at one another.

The next morning, when Jack woke, he grabbed Blue and raced into Mum and Dad's bedroom. He couldn't wait to find out who had come and had dinner with them last night. However, he didn't have to ask when he and Blue saw just who was sitting on the end of his mum and dad's bed.

It was Rose the teddy bear!

Blue looked at Rose who gave him the biggest smile ever.

4
BLUE'S SCHOOL ADVENTURE

Blue often thanked his lucky stars for the day he came into Jack Foster's life. Blue's life since then had changed so much by having lots of memorable adventures with his friend.

One of his favourite adventures was going to school with Jack. Blue had been there with him many times in the past and loved it. Especially, as Jack had lots of friends that wanted to hold and play with Blue.

'Are you ready for school?' Jack asked Blue one Monday morning as Blue looked back at him, his eyes gleaming in anticipation of another fun filled day of adventure.

'Boys, hurry up, we haven't got a lot of time and we're going to be late. Have you got everything?" Mum shouted out to Jack and Tom.

'Just coming,' they shouted back, as they rushed into the kitchen to grab their packed lunches, before stuffing them into their school bags.

The school wasn't far from their home, and normally they walked there. Although they'd had to use the old 4 x4 when Jack's leg had been broken.

Walking down the country lane that their bungalow was on, the boys ran ahead. Blue's head was poking out of Jack's rucksack. With spring just around the corner and because of where he was, Blue could see so many new things.

He remembered once looking at a book while Jack was

naming some of the animals in it. Now Blue saw some baby lambs in the fields skipping and jumping as they ran round baaing to their mums. He also saw lots of different flowers and wondered what they were called.

Suddenly, he heard Jack asking his mum the name of some of them.

'What are those yellow and purple flowers called?' Jack said. Going over to one and bending down, he sniffed it.

'They are called Crocus and the tiny white ones are called Snow drops.' Mum said smiling at him, before carrying on.

'Come on now Jack, or else we'll be really late, and we don't want Mrs Ansell or Miss Turner to mark you and Tom down as absent, do we?'

Jack shook his head as he ran to catch up with Tom and his mum.

They made it to school just in time. Going into the playground, they heard the bell ringing, a signal for the children to go into their classrooms.

'Bye, boys, see you at 3pm,' Mum said bending down to give them both a kiss on the cheek.

What she didn't see as soon as she turned away, was Tom quickly wiping his cheek on his sleeve, as his friends teased him about having red lipstick there. He rushed inside, whilst Jack who had taken his backpack off and put it on the ground was still chatting excitedly to his friends, the twins Adam and Charlotte King.

Blue loved hearing them talk about their favourite television show, Dr Who; they were so engrossed in talking about the episode that had been on at the weekend, they didn't see Mrs Ansell, their teacher coming towards them.

'Didn't you hear the bell?' she said interrupting them, before raising her eyes above her glasses. They glanced back at her, before looking down at the playground again.

'Sorry, Mrs Ansell,' they all said as they rushed to pick up their bags. Jack picked up his bag, putting it on one shoulder and walked quickly into the classroom.

However just as the children got to the door, she spoke again.

'Jack, Adam, Charlotte, there's plenty of time for you to talk when it's break time, but not now. Now you have work to do, and you need to concentrate on that, especially, you Jack.'

Blue saw Jack's puzzled look, until Mrs Ansell spoke again.

'After registration, we will be doing our sums.'

Jack's face fell. Blue knew that maths was his least favourite subject. He knew that Jack could easily add numbers, but when it came to taking them away, and doing his times tables, he had trouble with them and just couldn't figure them out.

Blue looked at his friend and felt sorry for him. If there were something he could do to help him, he would. Like the last time, when Jack was taking away fourteen, he'd used Blue's paws to help him.

Jack with a sigh put his bag on his peg and hung his coat on top, not forgetting to take Blue out first. He was going to put him on his desk, but Mrs Ansell had other ideas.

'No toys on your desk please, Jack,' she said shaking her head at him.

Blue and Jack couldn't believe it!

'But, I always have Blue on my desk Mrs Ansell,' Jack said, his bottom lip starting to wobble.

'Not today please,' she said giving him a disapproving glance.

Jack turned back towards his bag and put Blue into the rucksack again, leaving Blue's head poking out.

Now what was Blue to do? How was he to help Jack with his sums?

Jack was thinking the same thing. He really needed Blue's help. And his pal hadn't let him down before. Now what was he going to do?

Blue saw Jack's face fall and felt sympathy for him as Jack sniffed back tears. Mrs Ansell took the registration and once that was done, she asked the children to get out their maths books.

'Today we are going to be looking at your four times tables. I will go round the classroom to see how well you all know them. This way I will know who did their homework. And, more importantly, who didn't!' she said giving all the children a stern glance.

Somehow Blue knew Mrs Ansell was going to find out that Jack hadn't done his homework. Suddenly, Blue felt guilty. He and Jack had had so much fun at the weekend playing, when he knew Jack should have been doing his homework. He'd seen Mrs Ansell give Jack his maths homework on Friday afternoon, and he should have made him do it.

Even Mum had asked if Jack had any homework, and Blue remembered how Jack had told a small white lie when he said all he had was his reading book. Jack loved reading and would sit and read to Blue at bedtime every night. Mum would listen too, and then mark down in his reading planner how much he had read, and if he had got stuck with any words.

Now Jack wished that he and Blue had told her the

whole truth, as they knew she would have gladly helped him. She wasn't there to help Jack now, and more importantly, neither was Blue.

'Right, Jack, would you like to start us off with the 4 times table?' Mrs Ansell spoke interrupting his thoughts.

'4 times 1 is 4,' he began.

Blue could see Jack starting to smile. Had he finally grasped his times table? Mrs Ansell nodded her head, as she encouraged him along.

Blue listened and thought everything would be alright. Jack seemed to have got it at last.

However, when Jack got to 4 times 8, he got stuck.

'4 times 8 is…is 35, no I mean it's um.'

Mrs Ansell tried to encourage him.

'Remember Jack, what are 4 times 7?'

But, by this time Blue could see that Jack had totally forgotten, because he started to stutter.

'It's…it's, it's… I can't remember,' he wailed and began to cry.

Blue saw Mrs Ansell get up and go to him. He heard her say, 'don't worry about it for the time being.'

Then she gave him a hanky, before bending down to his level, and quietly saying, 'I think when the bell goes for break, you and I should have a talk. Don't you?'

Blue saw Jack nod, as he realised that Jack knew he had been caught out. How mad would Mrs Ansell be with him?

The rest of the morning flew by; Blue could see everyone was working hard from their maths books. Although he also saw that Jack was still having trouble with his sums, as he had an anxious look on his face the whole time.

Suddenly it was break time. Jack heard the bell go and

quickly got up, going to his bag to retrieve Blue.

He pulled Blue from it and hugged him tight. Blue hugged him back, hoping that would help. At that moment, all Jack wanted was a cuddle from his pal and that was all that Blue wanted too. He remembered Jack's mum saying that cuddles make all your troubles go away, well Blue hoped it would work this time for his friend.

'Jack, can you come here please?' Blue heard Mrs Ansell asking him.

Jack walked towards her, clutching Blue tight and dreading the telling off he knew he was going to get. Blue felt really scared for him, but they were in for a surprise.

'Hello, Blue,' Mrs Ansell said smiling at him as Jack held him tightly in his arms. 'I think Jack missed your help this morning.' She glanced at the look of astonishment on Jack's face.

'Yes, Jack, I was wrong not to let you have your Blue bear on your desk this morning.'

Blue almost did a double take as Jack too opened his eyes wide in surprise.

'You see...' she said beckoning Jack towards her, 'I realised that when Blue sat on your desk, he wasn't just there as a decoration, but, that in fact he helps you very much with your work...especially, your sums!'

Jack nodded both his and Blue's heads in agreement.

'I have seen you struggle in the past doing your maths, but just last week I saw that when you were taking away, you used Blue's paws to help you. And I have to say I was very impressed,' she said smiling at them.

'Do you know why I didn't let you have Blue on your table today?'

At that, Blue could feel Jack trembling, before he shook his head.

'Well I will tell you, it was because I thought that having done your maths homework over the weekend, that you perhaps wouldn't need Blue's help. However, it looks like I was wrong,' she shook her head sadly.

Blue looked up at Jack, as Jack knew he had to say something.

'I'm so sorry, Mrs Ansell, but I didn't do any maths homework at the weekend.' Jack quickly bowed his head in disgrace and so didn't see her give a little smile, which Blue did, but which she hastily hid when Jack looked up again.

'Is that so?'

Jack nodded slowly.

'Well we'll talk about that in a minute. However, do you know I think I was mistaken today...'

At that Jack looked amazed.

'I should have let you have Blue on your desk; he is obviously not just your friend, but your helper too.'

Jack nodded looking at his pal he smiled.

'But, he won't be there all the time, so that is why it really is important that you do your homework!'

Jack nodded solemnly.

'I will. I promise that from now on I will do ALL my homework,' he said giving Blue a big squeeze.

And Blue knew that in future he would be helping Jack as much as he could with his sums. Although reading was important, so was doing sums, and writing and Blue knew that, and he was determined to help his friend out in any way he could.

Today, both Jack and Blue had learned a valuable lesson, in that playtime was good, but so was learning too.

5
BLUE AND THE REMOVAL VAN ADVENTURE

Blue was left sitting on the breakfast bar as Jack rushed to the bathroom to clean his teeth before school. He overheard Mum talking to Dad about the removal lorry that was parked next door.

'Old Mrs Mortimer told me she had sold her bungalow to a couple who have their grandson living with them. I wonder how old he is; and if he'll go to the local school with the boys,' Mum said.

Out of the window, Blue could see the men removing some more furniture from the back of the van and taking it inside.

'Stop being so nosy,' Dad said laughing at her.

'Oh heck, look at the clock. Come on boys, aren't you ready yet?' Mum shouted out to them.

'Just coming, Mum,' they chorused back.

As they got to the front door, Jack stopped. 'Wait, I forgot Blue.'

'Jack, we don't have the time, we're going to be late for school at this rate, and we don't want Mrs Ansell to be cross with us, do we?'

'Please…' he said, turning back into the house.

'Oh… okay, but do hurry.' Mum sighed.

Just a few moments later he was back, and in time to meet the new neighbours who were standing talking to his mum and Tom.

'Jack, this is Deliwe Mwamuka, her husband Eden and

their grandson, Tasara-Liam…

'But everyone calls him Taz,' Eden interrupted, winking and smiling at the boy.

'Hi, Taz,' Jack said looking hopefully at him.

Taz didn't answer; instead he hid behind his Nan's back.

'He's going to start at your school tomorrow, and will probably be in your class,' Mum said, smiling at Jack.

'Don't worry Taz is a bit shy,' his Nan said smiling down at Jack before looking back at Taz. 'And he's sad that he had to leave all his friends behind in Zimbabwe.'

'Where's Zimbabwe?' Jack asked.

'It's in Southern Africa,' Mum said, 'Look, I'm sorry, but we must get a move on or else we'll be really late for school.'

'No worries,' Eden said.

'Why don't you all pop over later on for a cup of tea and some cake, when I get back from work and the boys are home from school? That way we can get to know one another a bit better, and the boys will be able to talk to Taz about the school, and, try to put his mind at ease over being the new boy tomorrow.'

'That would be lovely, wouldn't it, Taz?' Deliwe said. 'By the time we've unloaded everything from the van, we'll probably be ready for some tea and cake.'

They waved goodbye as Mum and the boys rushed up the road.

Blue's head was sticking out of Jack's rucksack and he was staring at the little boy, who was still jutting out from behind his Nan and who was also staring intently back at him.

However, Blue didn't have time to think about Taz anymore, as they rounded the corner and were on the main road to the school. They got there with seconds to spare as they saw Mrs Ansell going out into the playground, just as the bell started ringing.

'Whew! That was close,' Mum said raising her eyes as she glanced at the boys.

'See you later, Mum,' Jack said as he turned and waved to her. Tom didn't give her a backward glance as he hurried over to his friends standing in the playground.

Molly Bucket and the twins Charlotte and Adam King rushed over to Jack.

'You're late,' they said to him.

'I know, but our new neighbours are moving in, and we stopped to say hello to them. There's a boy who's going to live there with his Nan and Granddad and he's coming to this school tomorrow. They've got funny names.'

'What…'

But, before the children could say anymore, Mrs Ansell was calling them into the classroom and they all trooped in. Jack hung his bag on his peg and was careful to remove Blue, taking him out and placing him on his desk.

Blue liked helping Jack with his school work, and now Mrs Ansell didn't mind that Blue sat there, as she knew just how much he helped Jack with his adding up and taking away. Between the two of them, they had worked very hard trying to solve all Jack's maths problems. Mrs Ansell was pleased at the progress they had made.

Before long it was break time, and Jack was eager to take Blue out into the playground and finally talk to his friends about Taz.

'Well what's the boy called? You said he had a funny name,' Adam said.

'He's called Taz and his Nan's called Deliwe and his

Granddad's name is Eden, and they are from Zimbabwe, in Southern Africa.'

'Wow, that's exciting. I can't wait to see and talk to him,' Charlotte said.

'I don't think he will talk a lot. When we met this morning and I said hello, he didn't say anything to me. His Nan said he was shy, and that he missed his friends back there in Zimbabwe.'

'That's sad. We will have to do something to make him feel better and glad he's here.'

'Did you show him Blue bear?' Molly asked looking at Blue who Jack held in his arms.

'No, I didn't get the chance as we were running late for school, but, after school today, they are all going to come round to my house. I'll be able to show Blue to him then. He might even have his own teddy bear,' Jack said suddenly smiling at his friends.

'Come on then, let's go and play before the bell goes,' Adam said pulling on Jack's arm.

After break, it was time for the children to get ready for their P.E. class, and then after that it was lunch time. The day seemed to pass by very quickly, and before they knew it, it was nearly time to go home.

Unexpectedly, the door to the classroom opened and in walked the head teacher, Mr Jones, with Deliwe and Taz. Mr Jones was talking quietly to them and pointing out things in the classroom.

Then he turned to Mrs Ansell.

'Mrs Ansell, I am sorry to interrupt you, but I wanted to introduce you to a new student Tasara-Liam, but he likes to be called Taz. He will be joining you in your classroom tomorrow,' Mr Jones smiled down at him, but Jack saw Taz quickly hide behind his Nan again.

'Taz comes from Zimbabwe, which is in Southern Africa,' Mr Jones said beaming at the children.

Mrs Ansell went forward and bent down to talk to Taz. She put her hand out to him and very slowly he pulled his own out to shake hers.

'It's lovely to meet you, Taz, and welcome to our school. I'm sure you will love it here. And I expect you will have lots of exciting stories to tell us about your home back in Zimbabwe,' she said, before standing up again.

The home bell went then and she turned back to the class.

'Before you all go children, I think it would be nice of you to say hello to Taz and make him feel welcome.'

At that all the children turned towards Taz and said hello. However, he still remained firmly behind his Nan, still not speaking.

After a few seconds of silence, Mrs Ansell dismissed them all.

'All right class, I think Taz is a little shy at the moment. We'll see him tomorrow. Now off you go home.'

Jack looked at Blue and said, 'I don't think Mrs Ansell is ever going to get Taz to talk to her… or anyone.'

Blue looked at Jack thinking the same thing. They were going to have to do something to make him talk he thought!

By the time Jack went out into the playground, Tom was there with Mum. She was talking to Deliwe, who by this time had finished her tour of the school. Taz was standing by her side, still not speaking. Jack could see Tom was trying to talk to him, but Taz wouldn't look at him.

Even on the walk home, when Jack tried to talk to Taz he wouldn't speak. That was until Taz saw Blue sticking out of Jack's rucksack.

'I like your teddy bear,' Taz said beaming almost from ear to ear.

'He's great isn't he? When we get home, I'll get him out and you can play with him if you like,' Jack said returning his smile.

Thank goodness for Blue, Jack thought. If anyone could get Taz to talk, then it looked like it was going to be Blue!

As they reached Taz's house the removal lorry was still there.

'Are you still moving furniture in?' Mum asked Deliwe.

'I think Eden and the men have just about finished. We had quite a lot of things shipped over.'

'Well how about you ask them all to come to ours and I'll get the kettle going and sort out some sandwiches and cakes for everyone?' Mum said.

'Mum, can me and Taz play out here with Blue?' Jack asked.

'Well, if it's okay with his Nan, then I can't see why not,' Mum said looking for confirmation from Deliwe.

'That's fine, but don't go anywhere near the delivery lorry,' Deliwe said.

'We won't,' they said.

Jack got Blue out of his rucksack and handed him to Taz.

'Do you want to come and see my room? And I can show you my favourite toy,' Taz said running inside the bungalow with Blue, as Jack followed him in.

Taz ran into his room and skidded to a halt. Jack was right behind him and almost collided with him.

'What's up?' he asked.

'All my things are still in the boxes, and I don't know where Tiger is.'

'Shall we open them up and see if we can find him?' Jack said hoping the toy would be in the first box, as he was desperate to get outside and play while the weather was still nice.

Unfortunately, Tiger was nowhere in sight. And after opening up several boxes without any luck, the boys gave up.

'What if your tiger's still in the back of the van and the men haven't got it out yet?' Jack said looking at Taz.

'Shall we go and look?' Taz asked Jack.

'Well your Nan said we weren't to go anywhere near the lorry.'

'If we're quick, she won't know. Come on,' Taz said urging Jack to follow him.

Taz went back outside again with Jack. He wasn't too sure about going into the back of the lorry, but Taz walked up the ramp, so eventually Jack went too. Once in there, they were fed-up to see there were no more boxes. There were some dust sheets covering something, so Jack put Blue down on the floor to help Taz take them off.

They were disappointed. It was only a broken table. And Taz remembered his Nan telling him the removal men were going to take it away and get rid of it for her. That also meant Tiger must be in one of the boxes they hadn't opened in his bedroom after all!

Just then Jack heard his mum calling.

'Jack, Taz come in, I've made you a drink of squash and there are some sandwiches and cake for you.'

Jack crept to the edge of the lorry and peeked out. He was relieved to see his mum had her back to them as she stood in the kitchen. He put his finger to his lips urging

Taz to keep quiet as he moved forward. Then they jumped down from the lorry and made their way indoors, just as the removal men came out.

'Here you go boys, take your food and drink into the lounge; Tom is playing with his X-box. I'm sure he won't mind if you want to have a go,' Mum said shooing them out of the way.

At the door the men turned around.

'Thanks for the tea and food,' they said to Mum, before they turned to Deliwe. 'And thanks Mr and Mrs Mwamuka for the tip. We'd better get a move on, if we are going to get the ferry from Fishbourne.' They went to the back of the lorry and closed the door.

Blue saw the door close, and rushed over. He tried banging on it, to get the men's attention, but once they started the engine, they couldn't hear him over the noise.

'Help, help, let me out.' He shouted as loudly as he could, but it was no use, as the lorry drove off. He was trapped. What was he going to do? Would he ever see Jack again?

Fifteen minutes later, the boys came back into the kitchen with their empty plates and glasses.

'Mum can we go back outside and play? Only we didn't get a chance before, because Taz was looking for his tiger.'

'No, not now, you and Tom have got to have baths, and then it will be supper time, before a bedtime story and lights out,' Mum said.

'Oh I wish I'd known you were looking for Tiger, because I got him out and put him in the kitchen when you were looking round the school with Nan,' Eden said.

All of a sudden Jack looked around their kitchen.

'Mum, where's Blue?'

'I don't know. You had him last, remember? You and Taz were playing outside with him.'

Jack ran to the front door.

'Where's the removal lorry gone?' he said rushing back when he saw it wasn't there.

'They're probably at the ferry by now,' Eden said.

'Oh no,' Jack said as his bottom lip started to wobble and tears ran down his face.

Mum walked over to him.

'Whatever is the matter?' she said bending down to him.

Jack looked at Taz as he bowed his head.

'It was me, I was looking for Tiger and thought he might still be in the back of the lorry, so we went in there looking for him.'

On hearing that, Deliwe tutted and shook her head.

'Jack put Blue down on the floor to help me pull the blankets off the old table in there. I'm sorry, I know you told us not to go in there, but I wanted my Tiger,' Taz said, before he too burst into tears, looking really unhappy.

Deliwe shook her head again, but she went forward and pulled him into her arms to cuddle him.

'Don't cry, Taz, I'm sure it will be alright,' she said looking over his head at Mum.

But then Mum spoke.

'I don't know if we'll be able to get Blue back.'

At hearing that, Jack burst into uncontrollable sobs.

'I…I want my Blue back.'

'Hang on a minute. I have Len the driver's mobile number here. Let me see if I can get in touch with him,' Eden said, quickly pulling his mobile out and retrieving the number to ring him.

All the time Eden was on the phone, Jack was watching his face intently, hoping and praying that he had some good news about Blue. When Eden finished, he looked at them all with a smile on his face.

'Well, we were really lucky. They were just about to be loaded onto the ferry when I called. Len got Howard to get out and have a look in the back of the lorry, and they found Blue sitting right by the back door. He said if he didn't know better, it was almost as if Blue had been banging on them. Apparently he was found with his arms raised up.'

At that Jack looked at Taz and shrugged his shoulders. He hadn't left Blue by the doors, but he supposed with the lorry moving, it must have knocked him to the back.

'Anyway, they have given him to the people at the Wightlink terminal and the staff there said they will keep hold of him for you, until someone can pick him up.'

'Can we go, Mum?' Jack said heading towards the door.

'No, not now we can't. Don't forget Dad's got the car, because his work's van's off the road. He won't be back till later.'

'But, Mum,' Jack said before bursting into tears again.

'No buts. You were told not to go into the back of that lorry, and you disobeyed and went in there. I know Taz did too, and now you will have to learn from your mistake,' Mum said fishing a hanky out of her pocket and handing it to him. 'I promise you he will be alright. Knowing Blue, he will love all the fuss and attention he'll get from all the Wightlink staff, and Dad's working over in Ryde tomorrow, so I'll get him to go and collect Blue then.'

'I think you owe Jack an apology Taz,' Deliwe said

looking at him as he nodded.

'I'm sorry you lost Blue. When we go to school tomorrow, I'll take my tiger so you can play with him if you want,' Taz said.

Jack slowly nodded, before saying, 'What am I going to take to bed with me tonight now?'

Mum sighed and said, 'I tell you what, how about I ring Wightlink and you talk to the staff there. I'm sure they will put your mind at rest about Blue. And by the time you come home from school tomorrow, he will be here.'

Again Jack nodded, but still felt very sad.

'Right, it's time we got going and left you in peace,' Eden said as he, Deliwe and Taz went out of the front door.

'Come on; let's ring the terminal, shall we?'

After getting through, Jack spoke to a lady there.

'I've got your Blue bear here, he's so sweet,' she said tickling Blue under the chin.

'Will…will you look after him for me, please? My daddy's going to come and get him tomorrow,' Jack said sadly.

'I promise you, we will look after him. I will keep him safe on top of my desk, and sitting up there he can watch all the Wightlink ferries coming and going.'

Feeling slightly happier, Jack rang off.

'Bath time boys,' Mum said, as Jack forlornly followed her.

'While you boys are getting dressed, I'm just going to ring Dad to see when he will be home,' said Mum going into the lounge.

Later on when Dad came in Mum was reading Jack and Tom a bedtime story.

'And then the little panda…'

'Hey you haven't started the bedtime story without…'

'Blue,' Jack shouted out, jumping up off the bed as quickly as he could, as Dad produced Blue from inside his jacket.

Jack grabbed hold of his friend hugging him tightly to his chest. 'I didn't think you were going to get Blue back for me until tomorrow?' Jack said.

Dad looked at Jack cuddling Blue and smiled. 'You were very lucky, as when Mum rang me, I was already over in Ryde talking to my customer, Michelle Angell, about what I shall be doing in her garden tomorrow, so it wasn't a problem for me to pop by and collect him.'

'Look, the Wightlink staff put a sailor's hat on Blue's head,' Tom said pointing to it.

'Thank you, Mum and Dad,' Jack said smiling at them.

'Well perhaps next time you will do as you're told, but, for now, we'll say no more about it. Come on then, let's get this bedtime story read, then it's lights out,' Mum said giving Jack a sly wink.

Jack nodded; this was one night when he wouldn't argue about going to bed. He was just so happy to have his best pal back where he belonged safely in his arms.

6
BLUE'S SHOW AND TELL ADVENTURE

Jack was really happy as he walked to school with Blue in his backpack. His new friend and neighbour Taz, was with him. Taz had Tiger in his backpack. They were chatting away almost as if they had been friends forever, instead of only having met the previous day.

Jack's mum and Taz's nan were walking along behind the boys. As it was Taz's first day, his nan, wanted to make sure he was going to be alright, as the day before when he had looked around the school, he had been very nervous and anxious about going.

Suddenly, Jack stopped walking and got Blue out of the bag and gave him a cuddle. Blue loved being with Jack, it was the best thing in the whole world to be with his pal, especially as he was going back to school again. He was keen to help Jack in any way he could. If, by sitting on Jack's desk he could help him with his subjects as he watched Jack concentrate on getting them right, then that made him happy.

When they got to school, Taz went with his nan to the office while Jack and Tom waited in the playground for the bell to go. Jack went over to the twins, Adam and Charlotte.

'Hello, Jack and Blue,' Molly said stroking Blue on his soft head.

'Where is he then, the new boy?' Adam interrupted, looking behind Jack.

'He's had to go to the office with his nan, and I

suppose Mrs Ansell will collect him from there and then bring him to our classroom.'

Just then, the bell rang for them to go inside.

'Come on, Blue, let's go,' Jack said, placing him back in his rucksack again.

As they trooped into the classroom, there was Taz standing beside Mrs Ansell. For a second he looked worried, until he saw Jack, then he smiled at him.

'Jack, can you come here, please?' Mrs Ansell said, smiling at him as he made his way over to her with Blue in his arms.

'As Taz is your neighbour, and he told me he walked to school with you today, can you look after him?'

Jack looked at Taz and smiled before saying, 'Yes, Mrs Ansell.'

And then he said to Taz, 'Come this way, and I'll show you where you can hang your bag up.'

After finding Taz a spare coat hook, Taz noticing Blue in Jack's arms, took Tiger out of his backpack, before they went and sat down. After registration, it was Maths, which in the past, Jack used to dread, but since being allowed to have Blue on his desk for help, Jack found sums a lot easier.

'Taz, that's fine for you to have your tiger on your table. If he helps you in your subjects, as much as Blue helps Jack with his, then I don't mind,' Mrs Ansell said smiling at him.

At that Taz beamed at her, showing her his pearly white teeth.

The morning flew by and before too long; the bell was going for morning break. The children went to their lunch boxes to get out their healthy snacks. Jack got his apple and the twins got out their bananas, while Molly got out a satsuma. Jack was amazed when Taz produced some fruit he hadn't seen before.

'What's that?' Molly asked, looking warily at the fruit.

'It's guava, a fruit that comes from my country and I love it. I didn't think we would get it here, but my nan went shopping last night and was able to buy some. It's delicious; do you want to try it?' He asked them all, but the only one interested in trying any, was Jack.

'Taz is right, it's really nice. I bet you wish you could have some?' he said to Blue, as he wiped his face with the back of his hand.

But, Blue wasn't so sure!

They went and sat down on one of the benches in the playground and started eating their fruit. As Taz went to take another bit of his guava, Adam spoke.

'So where's your mum then?'

All eyes turned to Taz, as he stopped eating.

Jack looked at Blue and shrugged his shoulders. He didn't know anything about Taz's mum, so he too turned towards him, just as eager as the others to know all about her.

'My mum works as an air hostess, and her boyfriend lives in Portsmouth. He's a pilot. That's why we came to live here. I live with Nan and Granddad, because Mum travels a lot,' he said as he carried on eating his fruit.

'Where's your dad then?' Molly asked.

Taz shrugged his shoulders and bowed his head, before mumbling, 'he's still in Zimbabwe, but I never saw much of him anyway. I've always lived with Nan and Granddad, and he didn't come to see me when we lived there.'

Jack and Blue could see Taz looking unhappy, so Jack said, 'let's go and play before the bell goes and we have to go back inside for lessons again.'

At that Taz looked up quickly, and nodded.

Ten minutes later the bell went and the children went back inside to find it was their art lesson. They were painting pictures of the village. Jack was painting, Westmead Teddies, the teddy bear shop, and because Taz was new to the class, he had been asked to help Jack with his picture. Some children were painting the church, whilst others were painting the Post Office. The rest of them were painting the various shops, pubs and tea rooms, the village had.

There was going to be a mural of the whole village, which was going to be displayed in the hall. And then the local newspaper, The County Press, was coming to take pictures of it, to put in the paper. The paper was advertising the island as a holiday destination and the school thought it a great idea to let holiday makers know just what the village of Godshill, was like and what it had to offer.

Jack had Blue by his side; he stuck his tongue out as he concentrated hard on painting the windows of the shop.

'Jack, be careful you don't get paint on Blue,' Mrs Ansell said. 'It might be hard getting it off him again.'

'I won't,' Jack said, as he put his paintbrush down before going over to the odds and bods box, finding an old tee shirt.

Jack put the tee shirt on Blue and when he'd finished wrapping his pal up, all you could see were Blue's eyes. Blue was just glad Mrs Ansell had reminded Jack to cover him. Taz looked over at him and giggled.

'Well you won't get any paint on Blue now?' Taz said, as he turned to Blue and said, 'What colour is the door, Blue?'

Blue was looking at the paints on the table, and trying to indicate toward the brown, which was hard to do from inside the tee shirt.

'Brown; is that what you think?' Taz said, as he put his paint brush in the colour.

'That's great; how did you know that's the right colour?' Jack said, as he continued painting his windows.

'Blue told me,' Taz replied.

When the lesson finished, it was time for lunch. Afterwards, the afternoon seemed to fly by. Just before the home bell went, Mrs Ansell spoke to all of the children.

'As you have all been working really hard lately, I thought it would be nice to have a 'show and tell' afternoon. We will have it on Friday, I would like to choose…'

When Blue heard this, he hoped very much that it was he and Jack who would be chosen. Show and tell was Blue's favourite time at school. This was where the children took something into school that they loved, and they showed it to the other children, telling them all about it.

'Jack, and Taz because he's new to the school, to bring something in for show and tell. We will be having it just after afternoon break,' she said smiling at them both.

Jack put his hand up.

'Yes, Jack?' Mrs Ansell asked.

'Is it alright if I talk about Blue?' Mrs Ansell nodded and smiled at him.

'That's fine. I know you've told a lot of the children how you got him, but I've never heard the story, so would love to know all about it.'

Blue was really pleased; he couldn't wait for Friday afternoon to arrive now.

The rest of the week passed quickly, and before they knew it, it was Friday afternoon and show and tell time. When Jack came back in from break time with the other children, he had a shock, as standing with Mrs Ansell was Taz's nan, Deliwe.

'Children, if you would like to sit in a circle then we will begin our show and tell,' she said as they all sat down on the floor staring at Deliwe.

Then Mrs Ansell turned and looked at Jack.

'I've got a seat here for you and Mrs Mwamuka, so if you would both like to sit down, then Jack; you can start our show and tell, by telling us all what you have brought here today.'

Jack proudly held Blue in front of him.

'This is Blue, my bear,' he said holding him high, 'and when I was in hospital, I woke up on Christmas morning, and found him on the end of my bed. Father Christmas had brought him for me.' He smiled at everyone. 'I love my Blue, and when I told Mum I was going to do a show and tell about him, she thought it might be a good idea to find out where Blue came from.'

At the children's puzzled glances, he explained. 'Anna at Westmead Teddies shop thought Blue looked very old and could possibly even be a Michtom bear, although she doesn't think that is very likely, so we looked on the internet and read how Michtom bears were first made.' With that, Jack gave Blue to Adam.

'You can look at Blue and then pass him around to the others?' Jack said as he then started to read from a piece of paper he had on his lap.

'The people who invented the teddy bear, were a Mr and Mrs Michtom. My Mum and I found out that teddy bears are called after President Theodore Roosevelt, who

Mr and Mrs Michtom got permission from to call their bears, teddies, after the President's name.'

At this Jack stopped reading and smiled at Blue, who was being cuddled by Molly.

'We think my Blue is very old. He was made a very long time ago. My Mum and I think it might have been almost one hundred years ago?'

'Wow, that's really old,' Adam said looking at Charlotte as she nodded at him.

'Molly, can you please carry on passing Blue around?' Mrs Ansell reminded her.

'Oops, sorry,' Molly said, passing him on to Taz.

Jack continued. 'Mum, says because Blue's so old, I have to be careful with him, but Blue's my pal and he would hate not going everywhere with me. Wouldn't you Blue?' Jack said hugging his pal as Taz gave him back to him. 'He's not just a toy, he's my friend and we have many adventures together. That's why I love bringing him to school with me.' Jack beamed at Blue before looking at Mrs Ansell.

'Well that's really interesting, and well done to you and your Mum for finding out all that information about how Michtom bears came about. He really is a lovely bear, and you wouldn't think he was almost one hundred years old, he looks almost brand new,' Mrs Ansell said. 'Thank you Jack, and now we'll let Mrs Mwamuka talk. Children, when I told Taz he could bring anything in to show and tell, he decided he wanted to bring his nan here today to talk about the village where they used to live and what it was like for them? Especially for Mrs Mwamuka when she was growing up?'

Jack looked at Blue. They were both interested to hear what Taz's nan had to say.

'When Taz came home and told me about the wonderful paintings you are all doing of the village, I started telling him all about our village and what it was like when I was a little girl living there, although not a lot has changed since then,' she said looking at Taz and smiling.

'Anyway he wanted me to come here today and tell you all about it. Perhaps I should start off by telling you the name of it, it is called Murewa.' She looked at the children and said, 'can you say Murewa?'

Molly tried saying the name, but got stuck.

So Deliwe said to her, 'If you break the word down and say Mu...re ...wa, you should get it.'

Molly did as she was told and was really pleased when she pronounced the name correctly. Soon all of the children were saying it properly.

'Well done,' Deliwe said, smiling at them. 'In our village, there are about thirty huts. They all have thatched roofs, which are very similar to some of the thatched cottages here in the village. The only difference is that our huts are round, and they have no electricity in them.'

'No electric. Does that mean you don't have any televisions?' Adam blurted out as Mrs Ansell looked at him.

'Adam, please don't shout out?'

'That's alright, Mrs Ansell, I expect it is very strange for the children to know there is a village that doesn't have electricity. And, I have to say, that in our country this isn't unusual. A lot of small villages have no power, but we managed all the same. We had candles and oil burners to use at night.'

Adam was shaking his head and whispering to Jack.

'No television? That means they can't have x-boxes or

any sort of games consoles?'

Mrs Ansell shushed them.

'Boys, please be quiet and let Mrs Mwamuka speak.'

Deliwe nodded.

'The round parts of the huts are our kitchens and we use the fireplaces in them to do any cooking. Next door is the bedroom, where many people sleep on camp beds and that is all that the huts have in them.'

Blue thought how lucky he was to sleep in Jack's bed with him. It was so comfortable, the camp beds didn't sound too comfortable though.

Jack raised his hand.

'Where are your bathrooms then?' he said, looking at the others.

Deliwe smiled and shook her head.

'No we didn't have bathrooms. We used latrines, which are our toilets, and are a hole in the ground.'

'Oww, yuck,' Molly and Charlotte said, until Mrs Ansell told them to be quiet.

'That's enough now, please let Mrs Mwamuka continue with her very interesting story.'

'The thing is girls, we didn't know anything different. And it would be impossible to install a plumbing system. Although; I must admit it is lovely having a bathroom here.' She smiled at them, before turning to Taz and saying, 'isn't it Taz?'

'Yes, I love having a shower indoors, so much better than having buckets of cold water thrown over me?' He laughed.

The girls looked curiously at Taz.

'Nan, tell everyone where we got our water from?'

'We used to get our water from boreholes, which are very similar to wells. And we used this water to wash with too.'

At this, the children's eyes were almost out on stalks.

'You mean the water didn't come out of a tap?' Adam asked, as Deliwe shook her head.

'No, we had a pump to get it out of the ground. And every day we'd go there to fill our buckets up. Even the children of the village would have to go with their buckets to fill them with water.'

At that, everyone turned towards Taz.

'Did you do that then, Taz?' Jack asked him.

'Yes, but my bucket wasn't that big. So I would have to go back quite a few times,' he said smiling at them.

Wow! Blue found that really interesting.

Charlotte put her hand up.

'Can I ask, what's your food like? Only when Taz came to school the other day, he had a funny looking piece of fruit. Jack tried some and he liked it.'

At that Jack nodded, 'Yes, it was yummy.' He rubbed his tummy as everyone else laughed.

'We normally eat something called sadza. It's a bit hard to describe what it tastes like. I will make some and get Taz to bring it in, so you can try it. Would you like that?'

The children nodded.

Mrs Ansell said, 'Perhaps, we can have a day, where we can all bring in one of our favourite foods.'

'That would be brilliant,' Jack said to Blue, 'I could get Mum to cook my favourite pudding, Banoffee pie.'

'Quiet now please, Jack!' Mrs Ansell said, 'Let's let Mrs Mwamuka carry on, or else the bell will go for home time and we won't have heard everything she has to tell us.'

'We planted seeds to grow our own vegetables, and we had fruit trees, where we grew lemons and avocados.

They were a lot bigger than the ones you get in this country.' She chuckled. 'We got milk from our cows, and often, we had chickens, which roamed the house and the kitchen,' she said smiling at their puzzled faces.

'Any other food we wanted, we'd have to travel to our local town which was roughly thirty miles away. There were two buses each day, one to get us there, and one to bring us home again. If we missed the bus back, then we had to use our feet and walk.'

The children looked at one another in amazement.

'Walk all that way?' Molly said to Charlotte raising her eyes, as Deliwe nodded.

'Nan, tell everyone about the school there,' Taz said.

'Well, when I was a little girl, I didn't go to school until I was seven years old…'

Jack looked at Blue and said, 'Cor, I wish that happened here!'

The other children heard what he said and laughed, even Mrs Ansell smiled.

'Ah yes Jack, as I said that was the age when I was a child, but recently they have reduced it to six.' Deliwe smiled at the face he made.

'Also, we don't have a church in our village, not like the lovely old church you have here. So we regularly used the school for our church services,' she said swiftly looking over at the clock on the wall and seeing it was nearly home time.

'When I was a child, we used to play games like you play in your playground. Our version of hopscotch is called Pada, and we also played a pebble game called Nhodo. I expect Taz can show you how to play it,' she said looking at him as he nodded.

'Can I ask do you have a traditional dress?' Mrs Ansell

asked.

'We don't have one, but some of our neighbouring countries do. They wear brightly coloured tops and skirts, which have really rich vivid colours.'

Mrs Ansell nodded, as she too glanced at the clock on the wall.

'Well children, I think we should say a great big thank you to both Jack and Mrs Mwamuka for making our show and tell afternoon so informative. Can we give them a round of applause?'

At that all the children clapped as Deliwe and Jack, who was hugging Blue, stood up.

Jack turned to Taz and said, 'I'm so glad you brought your nan here today, it was great hearing all about your country. I expect you miss it, but hopefully, you will grow to love living here just as much.'

'I was missing my friends, but because now I have you and Blue as friends, I don't think I'm going to miss them as much anymore,' Taz said as he smiled at Jack and Blue, who beamed back at him.

7
BLUE'S PICNIC ADVENTURE

Jack and his friends rushed out into the playground, laughing and chattering away with one another.

'Bye, see you Tuesday,' Molly Bucket called out to Jack and Blue as she ran to her mum's car.

Jack waved to her and then walked over to his mum.

'It's brilliant, we're off on Monday,' Tom said.

'Yes, it is,' Jack replied smiling at his mum as she pulled a face.

'That Bank holiday Monday has sure come round quickly?' she said.

'Mum, if it's nice and sunny, can we go to the seaside?' Jack asked. 'And, can we take a picnic too? Blue's never been to the seaside, or had a picnic before, have you?' Jack said looking at his pal.

'Well, I would hate to disappoint Blue, so it looks like it's going to be the beach and a picnic on one of the days this weekend,' she said laughing.

Jack started dancing around with Blue in his arms.

'It's a shame Taz isn't here. He could have come with us,' Jack said to Blue.

His mum interrupted him, 'Oh, but it's the first time he's got to see his mum, since moving to the island. His nan was picking him up and taking him straight to the hovercraft to go and meet her in Southsea.'

'I know, but it would have been fun to take him to the beach too.'

'Well, we do live on an island surrounded by water,

and now the good weather's here, we should be able to go lots of times. And, of course Taz can come with us sometimes,' Mum said smiling at him.

'Okay,' Jack said smiling happily.

'Race you to the end of the path,' Mum suddenly shouted out to the boys, as she flew past them.

'Hey, that's not fair, you cheated,' Tom shouted laughing at her as he and Jack ran to catch up.

Sadly, the next morning the weather was not good; rain clouds hovered overhead.

'It looks like we won't be going to the beach today,' Mum said when the boys came for breakfast.

'Oh!' Jack moaned, putting Blue down on the breakfast bar besides his bowl of cereal.

'I know it's a shame, but don't forget, if we can't go today, we've got tomorrow or Monday, providing the weather's a lot better than it is at the moment.'

By now, it had started raining really heavily; the water was hitting the windows very hard.

'So what are we going to do?' Tom asked looking at the rain.

'Well I can get the paints out after breakfast and you can do some painting.'

Jack and Tom shook their heads.

'Boring!' they both said together.

'What about playing with your toys?' Mum said shrugging her shoulders helplessly.

'Boring!' Jack and Tom said again.

'Well I don't know what to suggest. All I know is that I don't want you watching the television or playing on your games console all day.'

'But, Mum,' Tom pleaded.

'No, buts, I know you boys, if you had your way, that's

what you would end up doing all day. So, NO telly and NO games console, at least not until later on, perhaps this afternoon.'

Tom finished his breakfast and skulked off back to his bedroom.

'So what are you and Blue going to do?' Mum asked Jack.

'Could we get all the things we need for the picnic, so if it's nice tomorrow, we can just get them and go.'

'Yes, I can't see why not. Look, let me clear the breakfast things, and whilst I'm doing that, can you go to the airing cupboard and get out the big blue and white square checked tablecloth? We can use that to sit on at the beach.'

Jack nodded and finishing his cereal, he tipped his bowl forward scooping up the milk into his spoon, before slurping it into his mouth.

'Ahh, that feels better,' he said smiling at Blue and wiping his mouth with the back of his hand.

Holding Blue tightly in his arms, he went to the airing cupboard. Opening the door to the cupboard, he saw the table cloth that Mum had told him to get. However, it was at the top, on the highest shelf.

'I think the only way we're going to get the cloth is for me to climb up there,' Jack said, placing Blue down on the floor.

Blue looked at the shelves and didn't think they looked very safe. He hoped Jack would be alright.

'This is easy, Blue,' Jack said as he climbed on the lowest shelf, before pulling himself up to the next one.

There were only a couple more to go before he got to the top. But, just as Jack reached the top shelf and the table cloth, he lost his grip and fell, bringing the table cloth tumbling down on top of him and covering Blue as well.

'Jack!' Mum cried out, rushing to him after hearing the crash. She pulled back the table cloth.

Jack was cuddling Blue and laughing.

'That was fun!'

'Fun! You scared the living daylights out of me. I thought you'd broken your leg again,' Mum said, laughing despite herself.

Jack giggled.

'This is fun, isn't it, Blue? It's like being in a tent.'

'A tent you say. Hey that gives me an idea,' Mum said smiling at him and Blue and winking.

She scooped the table cloth off them.

'Hey, I was having a great time with that.'

'Go and get your brother and then come into the kitchen,' Mum said taking the table cloth with her.

Jack got up and wandered towards his brother's bedroom.

'Tom, Mum wants us to go into the kitchen,' Jack said.

At the door, he came to a sudden stop.

'Mum said you weren't to play on your PlayStation.'

'Sssh, keep your voice down. I don't want Mum to hear. And, don't you go telling on me,' Tom said, looking at his brother before turning back around to his game.

'But, Mum said…'

'Leave me alone,' Tom shouted out.

'Come on, Blue, let's go back to the kitchen,' Jack said sadly to his pal as they turned and left Tom to his game.

'Where's Tom?' Mum asked when he wandered in to the kitchen again.

Jack just shrugged his shoulders.

'He's playing in his room,' he said, hoping that Mum wouldn't go and look. Jack didn't want Tom to think he had told on him, dobbing him in.

Mum nodded.

'Dah da, what do you think?' she said, moving aside so Jack and Blue could see what she had done.

'Mum, it's great,' Jack said as he and Blue made their way over to the table, that wasn't just a table any longer.

It was a den! Mum had placed the chairs around the table and draped the huge table cloth over all of them, pegging the cloth to the chairs with some clips, to keep it in place. She'd weighed the table cloth down with some of her weights from her old scales. Then she'd got all the cushions from the lounge, scattering them on the floor, to make it comfortable.

'I thought you, Blue and Tom could play in there, and later we could make some cakes for our picnic. What do you think of that?'

'That's cool.' Jack beamed at her. 'I'm going to my room to get some of my toy cars.'

'Okay, you go and do that, while I get the ingredients out of the cupboard for the cakes,' Mum said going towards the kitchen whilst Jack and Blue went back to his bedroom.

When they came back again, Mum had all the ingredients ready for making some cup-cakes. She had wrapped a tea towel around her waist and she was holding one up for Jack. Sitting on the side was one of Dad's clean handkerchiefs, which she held up for Jack to wrap around Blue's waist.

'We'll make chefs of you two yet,' she said laughing as Jack tied the handkerchief. Where's your brother? I've got a tea towel ready for him too.'

Jack shrugged his shoulders and shook his head.

'Right, if you wash your hands…'

Jack went to the sink.

'I won't be a minute. I'll go and get him,' Mum said as she turned around, going towards Tom's room.

'Mum…' Jack called after her, but she'd disappeared around the corner.

He winced when he heard her telling Tom off.

'What did I tell you, Tom? You have deliberately disobeyed me. Right turn that off… NOW!'

Jack heard his brother arguing with Mum, before she came back into the kitchen with Tom trailing behind her.

'You're a tell-tale,' Tom shouted at Jack.

'Tom, stop that now. Jack didn't say a word; all he told me was that you were playing in your room.' She looked at Jack shaking her head at him.

'Sorry, Mum,' Jack said.

'It's not you who should be apologising!' she said turning and looking at Tom.

'Sorry, Mum,' he said looking at her, before turning sheepishly to Jack. 'Sorry, Jack.'

'Right, if you wash your hands, and then come over here, I will put this tea towel on you and we can all make some cup-cakes. How does that sound?' Mum said smiling at the boys.

Once Tom's hands were clean, he, Jack and Blue stood beside Mum watching what she was doing.

'Right, first off we have to weigh the flour out. Tom, can you carefully pour some of the flour into the bowl, and then Jack you can place it on the digital scales.'

'Okay, Mum,' Tom said, pouring the flour into the bowl. 'Here, Jack, you carry it over to the scales.'

Jack walked over to the scales, and put Blue down on the side. He was sticking his tongue out as he concentrated on not spilling any of it, as he put it down onto the scales.

'Well done boys. Tom you poured the right amount in, and Jack you got the bowl to the scales without spilling any of it,' Mum said. 'I'll keep this bowl, and then Jack, can you scoop some butter out of the dish, and put it into this bowl here?' she said handing him another one, 'and Tom you can weigh it for me?'

'Yes, Mum,' Jack said taking the bowl back to the side and picking up the wooden spoon, he dug out some butter from the dish, putting it into the bowl.

'You'll need 125gms, and once you have it, Tom can bring it over here and I'll add it to my mixing bowl.'

Once that was done Mum took the bowl from Tom.

'Now, Blue and I will weigh out the caster sugar.'

'You and Blue?' Jack said excitedly.

'Yes, me and Blue. You didn't think you and Tom were going to bake the cakes all by yourselves, did you?'

Mum laughed as she picked Blue up holding one of his paws, she placed a dessert spoon in it and together they weighed out the right amount of sugar. Afterwards she and Blue carried it over to the mixing bowl.

'Now for the fun part,' she said looking back at the boys as she began creaming the sugar and butter together.

'Right, can you both gently put some flour in to the mixture? If you put one spoonful in first Tom, I'll fold it in, and then Jack can have a go. We'll do it like that, until there's no flour left.'

'What about Blue? When's it his turn?' Jack said.

'Oh, sorry, Blue, silly me,' Mum said going forward and picking Blue up as she helped him with the dessert spoon, putting some of the flour into the mixing bowl and folding it in with the sugar and butter.

'Blue's had his go, now it's your turn,' Mum said

holding the spoon out to the boys.

They carried on adding the flour to the mixture, until it was all gone.

'Jack, can you put the cake cases out on the baking tray please? And then you can all...including Blue, spoon, the mixture into the cake cases.'

'After, can we lick the bowl out?' Jack asked excitedly.

Mum nodded, 'Yes.' She laughed.

Once that was done, and the boys were busy licking the bowl out, Mum took the cakes to the oven. She'd turned it on earlier, putting the dial to the right temperature, before she put the cakes in.

'I'll set my timer for twenty minutes, and we'll see how the cakes are doing? They might want a couple more minutes, so we will check them then. And then once they are done, and cooled down, we can make some butter icing and you can decorate them with some edible decorations.'

'Yippee, I can't wait to taste them. I wish you could eat one Blue,' Jack said squeezing his pal tightly.

'Do you boys want to go and play in your den while the cakes are cooking?'

The boys nodded and went to the den. For a while they played with the cars Jack had fetched earlier and then, before they knew it, the timer went off.

'Can we come and see the cakes?' Jack said, picking Blue up and walking over to the oven.

'Yes, I'll open the door, but stand back, because of the steam coming out of it. I don't want you to burn yourselves,' Mum said as she opened the door carefully.

'They look great,' Tom said, looking over Jack and Blue's shoulders at them.

'Yes, I think they are done. Just let me put a knife in

and see if the cake springs back up.'

After sticking the knife in, Mum told them they were done.

'I'll leave them here on the side to cool down, and turn off the oven. You boys can go back to your game for a while, and then we can decorate them.'

'Cool,' Jack said.

While the boys were playing, Mum made up some butter icing. She added blue food colouring to it. Once the cakes were cool enough, she called the boys back over.

'I've done this one to show you what you can do with the icing. Do you think Blue will like it?'

The boys looked at the cake she'd decorated. By fluffing up the icing and adding chocolate Smarties for the eyes and the nose, the cake looked just like Blue's face!

'Mum, that's great,' Jack said looking at Blue to see the resemblance.

'Well, when you said Blue couldn't have any of the cakes to eat, I thought perhaps he could be on them instead.'

'That's fab, Mum. Can you show us how you did that?' Jack asked as Tom nodded and Mum gave each of the boys a cake, showing them exactly what she'd done.

When they'd finished decorating the cakes, they went back to the den to carry on playing. Lunchtime was coming up, so Mum decided to make some sandwiches. She made a drink for them all, and carrying the sandwiches, drinks and a cake for each of them on a tray, she made her way over to the den.

'Here we go,' she said bending down with the tray and entering the den. 'As we can't have a picnic outside, I thought perhaps we could have one in the den. What do you say to that?'

'Cool,' both boys chorused as they grabbed a sandwich and started eating it.

'I'm sorry boys, but I've just heard the weather forecast for the next couple of days, and it looks like this rain is going to be staying around. So I don't think we'll be able to go to the beach for a picnic, well not this weekend.'

'That's alright, Mum. This picnic is way better, and at least we won't get sand in our sandwiches,' Jack laughed, hugging his pal close, as he picked up his cake to take a bite from it.

8
BLUE'S GREAT EASTER EGG HUNT ADVENTURE

Jack and his brother Tom, were getting all excited, but Blue wasn't sure what about. They were talking about going on a Great Easter Egg Hunt. Whatever that was. From Friday, they would be on school holidays for two weeks.

At playtime, Blue had heard Jack's school friends talking to him.

'Are you going on the Great Easter Egg Hunt?' Molly Bucket asked the small group of children standing there.

'Yes we are. I can't wait to go and look for all the Easter eggs. I hope I get more than I got last year,' Adam said to his sister Charlotte, before they turned and looked at Jack and Blue.

Jack nodded. 'Tom and I are, AND... my Nannie and Grandpops are coming all the way from Yorkshire for Easter, so they'll be coming too!' he said excitedly swinging Blue around in a circle.

So the Easter egg hunt was looking for eggs, Blue thought. He was also intrigued, as to who Nannie and Grandpops were.

However, once at home, Blue solved that mystery, when he overheard Dad asking Mum if she had heard from her parents.

'Do you think your Mum and Dad will be able to make it down from Yorkshire, or is your Mum's leg still playing her up?' Dad asked.

'Well, it was ironic that she should break her leg at near enough the same time as Jack broke his.' Mum shook her head.

Blue heard Dad say, 'I know, her leg won't heel as quickly, so perhaps we shouldn't push them into coming down. How about, instead, we have them come down for a couple of weeks in the summer. That way the weather will be warmer, and I might be able to get some time off work too. What do you say to perhaps putting them off till then?'

'Yes, I suppose so… although both the boys will be so disappointed. And are you so sure that you'll be able to get two weeks off in the summer?' Mum said, giving Dad a small grimace as he shrugged his shoulders.

Blue saw the sad look on Mum's face as she telephoned her parents that evening putting them off from making the trip down to the island. He felt really sorry for her, especially when she told the boys the bad news.

'But, Nannie and Grandpops didn't come at Christmas. And I wanted to show them Blue, and we really wanted them to help us in the Great Easter Egg Hunt!' Jack moaned to Mum.

'I know, and they very much wanted to come too, but it's such a long way from where they live. Grandpops doesn't like driving now, so it would have meant them having to come by train. It's too much for them; especially with Nannie's leg still playing her up, plus having to cope with their luggage as well,' Mum said, gently ruffling Jack's hair.

'Hey, did you tell Blue that where Nannie and Grandpops live, it was made famous by The Bronte sisters?' Mum said trying to cheer him up.

'I don't know who they are,' Jack replied so Mum tried

again.

'How about as they can't come down to us, we go up to them sometime? We could always take Blue on the Keighley and Worth Valley steam railway. You could show Blue, the movie, 'The railway children,' as that's where they filmed it.'

'I suppose so,' Jack said miserably.

Blue upon hearing this thought really hard. Was there another way to get Jack's grandparents to the island for Easter and the Great Easter Egg Hunt, and more importantly, put smiles back on Jack and his mum's faces again?

Just as Mum was tucking Jack and Blue up in bed, Blue looked at the aeroplane wallpaper, 'of course,' he thought.

It wasn't long before Jack was fast asleep, and that's when Blue put his idea into Jack's head. He wriggled free from Jack's arms and pulled himself up onto his pillow. Leaning down towards his ear, he whispered in it, over and over again.

'What about Nannie and Grandpops flying down to the island?'

When he saw Jack's lips moving, repeating what he'd said, that's when he knew he had got it.

The next morning, almost before the sun was up Jack woke with a start. He jumped excitedly out of bed, grabbing hold of Blue before rushing upstairs into his parents' bedroom.

'Mum, Dad, I've had a great idea,' he said skidding to a halt just at the foot of their bed. Blue looked across at Rose and gave her a sly wink.

'Jack, it's only 5.30am. What are you doing up so early?'

'It's because I've had an idea on how Nannie and

Grandpops can come over to the island for Easter.'

At that Mum quickly struggled to sit up in bed.

'What idea?' she said turning on the light.

Now that Jack had both their attention, he continued.

'They could fly down to the island.'

'No they can't do that...' Dad said, before Mum interrupted him.

'No, they can't actually fly to the island... however, they could fly from Leeds Bradford Airport to Southampton's airport. And then, they could get a taxi to the fast Cat, bringing them over to Cowes, where we could pick them up. That's a brilliant idea Jack, what made you think of that?'

Jack looked mystified for a second.

'I don't know. It came to me in my dreams,' he said, before beaming at them both.

And so it was all arranged. Nannie and Grandpops were going to fly down after the boys broke up from school. Mum was especially pleased, as Dad always had holiday with them at Easter, and she knew he would have found it really hard trying to get two weeks off in the summer. He was a self-employed gardener, and his work always picked up by then.

On Saturday, when Nannie and Grandpops were due, Jack and Blue were busy counting down the time until they could finally go and collect them from the fast Cat.

'How much longer before we can go and pick them up?' Jack shouted out.

Give me five minutes, and then I'll be ready,' Mum said smiling at the eagerness on his face.

'I can't wait to show them Blue, and to tell them all about the Great Easter Egg Hunt tomorrow. It will be so exciting, Grandpops can go hunting with Tom, and

Nannie can come with me and Blue!'

'Well, we'll have to wait and see how tired Nannie and Grandpops are. And, more importantly, if Nannie will be up to trudging around, looking for eggs,' she said giving him a quick smile before picking up her car keys.

'Oh she will, won't she, Blue?' Jack said confidently to his friend.

'Come on then.' Mum said as she walked out to the car.

Blue wondered how they would all fit into the car, but Dad said he would to stay behind. There wouldn't be enough room in the 4 x 4 with all the luggage, Nannie and Grandpops would no doubt bring with them Dad had jokingly told Mum.

As soon as they pulled up in front of the terminal, Nannie and Grandpops were standing there waiting, with ALL, of their luggage. Jack looked at his mum and smiled, as she winked back at him.

'Nannie, Grandpops,' Jack shouted out as he rushed over to their sides.

'E by gum, Jack, let me look at you,' Nannie said enveloping him in a great big hug, before loosening her hold slightly to hold him at arm's length.

'Nannie, this is Blue, my bear that I was telling you all about,' Jack said thrusting Blue towards her.

'Well how do you do?' Nannie said shaking one of Blue's paws enthusiastically.

Blue liked her and Grandpops very much, as when he was introduced to Blue; Grandpops had also shaken his paw vigorously.

On the journey back to Godshill, Nannie and Grandpops told them all about their flight, and how much easier it was. More importantly, it was something they'd wished they had done a long time ago.

'Now that we know how much simpler it is, we will be able to do it all the time,' Nannie said as she sat at the kitchen table drinking a cup of tea. All the others nodded.

Easter Sunday, saw both boys rushing into their grandparents' bedroom early.

'Wake up, wake up, it's Easter,' They both shouted out as they jumped up and down on their bed.

'Calm down boys,' Nannie said smiling at the excitement on their faces.

'It's the Great Easter Egg Hunt today. You are coming aren't you?' Jack said looking hopefully at them.

'Of course we are,' Grandpops said, giving Nannie a sideways glance as he saw her look fondly back at the boys.

'Off you go now boys and get your breakfast, Grandpops and I will be out shortly,' Nannie urged them.

After breakfast, they all drove to Ventnor Botanic garden, where the Easter egg hunt was due to take place.

'Right, Nannie, Mum, Blue and me, will go hunting this way, and Grandpops, Dad and Tom, you can go the other way,' Jack said, pulling his Nannie on the arm and leading her off.

'Yeah, and I bet we beat you to the golden egg too,' Tom said pulling his Dad and Grandpops in the opposite direction.

'What's the golden egg?' Nannie asked as she slowed down and stopped walking. Blue was glad she'd asked, because he was also wondering what the golden egg was.

'Whoever finds the golden egg, wins a family day trip out to Havenstreet Steam Railway, and gets to go on a steam train,' Jack said happily looking at Blue's face.

That would be really exciting, Blue thought as he

remembered how he and Jack had watched the film, 'The Railway Children,' and how he'd loved seeing the steam train in that film.

'Well we'd better get a move on then, hadn't we?' Nannie said winking at Mum.

However, after looking around the park and finding many eggs, they hadn't found the golden one. There were lots of families all looking for that special egg too. By now, Nannie said she was starting to feel tired.

'Nannie, why don't you sit down on that bench and wait for us?' Mum said pointing to the nearby seat.

Jack looked at his Nannie, and suddenly felt bad. She did look tired; perhaps he shouldn't have demanded she come. Then, he had an idea.

'Yes, Nannie, why don't you sit and wait for us on the bench. Blue can sit with you and keep you company, can't you, Blue?' he said looking at his pal.

'Well, if you're sure, I could do with sitting down for a few minutes, and then Blue and I can come and find you.'

'No, you just sit here, and when we've had enough of egg hunting, we'll come back to you, won't we Jack?' Mum said and Jack nodded.

They left Nannie sitting on the bench by an old oak tree. It had fallen over in a recent storm, snapping almost completely in half. Just for fun, Jack had placed Blue on the edge of the trunk.

Suddenly, there was a gust of wind, and Blue fell inside the trunk.

'Help,' he cried out as he struggled to push himself up.

There were lots of leaves in the stump of the tree and where Blue had fallen in some of them had blown away. It wasn't very comfortable lying there; something was digging into his back. He moved some of the leaves out of the way and couldn't believe his eyes!

'So what do you say, Blue, you and I put our heads together to try and find out, just where that golden egg is hiding?' Nannie said turning around towards him.

But, he wasn't there!

'Oh no, oh my goodness, Blue where are you?' she said standing up and looking to see if he had fallen down on the ground. He was nowhere to be seen.

'Blue where are you?' Nannie shouted out.

'Nannie, what's the matter?'

Nannie slowly turned around. Standing there were Jack and Mum!

'What are you doing back here so quickly?' she asked.

'Well, Jack and I felt bad leaving you here all alone, so decided to come back and sit and wait with you for the others to come back. I texted Dad to tell him where we are, and anyway, Jack has loads of eggs,' she said smiling at Jack, but instantly the smile was gone.

'Nannie, where's Blue?' Jack said, his bottom lip started to wobble as he looked at the tree stump where he'd placed Blue, but he was no longer sitting there.

'Do you know, I think he's on the golden egg hunt,' Nannie said quickly, seeing the look of relief on his face. 'Shall we see if we can find him?' She said holding her hand out to him.

Jack nodded and went forward to take it. Then they both walked over to the stump of the tree. Lying just inside it was Blue...and he was lying on the golden egg!

'Blue found the golden egg, Nannie,' Jack said jumping up and down, before picking up Blue and the egg.

Just at that moment, Tom, Dad and Grandpops came over to them.

'We found loads of eggs, but we didn't find the golden

one,' moaned Tom, shaking his head.

At that Jack turned to him with a beaming and knowing smile as he held Blue and the golden egg up for them to see.

9
BLUE'S STEAM TRAIN ADVENTURE

Blue was excited, after finding the golden egg at the Easter Egg Hunt; it meant Jack's family had won a day out at Havenstreet Steam Railway, and the fact he, Blue, would be going on a steam train was really awesome. He couldn't wait for the day to come!

Jack was especially pleased, because his Nannie and Grandpops were still down from Yorkshire; so they were going with them. It was all arranged that they would go the following Saturday afternoon.

The day dawned bright and sunny, although it was still a little cold. Mum made sure the boys wrapped up tight in their scarves and hats, and Jack got Blue his scarf and hat too, wrapping him up firmly.

'Is everyone ready?' Dad said tapping the car keys on the side table.

'Yes, I think so,' Mum said looking at the others.

'Well let's get going then,' Dad said turning towards the door and striding outside.

'Nannie, you sit in the front with Dad, and Grandpops and I can sit in the back with the boys,' Mum said.

'I'd like that,' Nannie said smiling fondly at Dad, who nodded at her as they got to the car.

Blue sat on Jack's lap all the way there, while Mum did a running commentary about all the places they passed on their way to Havenstreet.

When they got to the road to turn off for the steam railway, Jack said, 'Mum, is that farm shop down there?'

'You've got a good memory, that's right, it is. It's called Bridlesford Farm and the café, is called Bluebells.'

'Do you remember when we went there and had something to eat, and afterwards we went and looked at the baby cows?'

Jack looked at Blue.

'Mum, do you remember that poor baby cow that broke its leg? It had to have a cast, just like us.'

Blue had a lot of sympathy for the calf. When he had first met Jack he'd been in hospital, with a badly broken left leg. The nurses had put a cast on Blue's left leg too, to make Jack feel better. And just a couple of days after having the cast removed, Jack had broken his right leg as well!

'Yes, I do. They have the calves in pens, just before you go into the café, and unfortunately one of them had broken its leg, when we went there. So they'd had to put a plaster cast on it.' Mum laughed at Jack's enthusiasm for the cows. Looking at Nannie, Mum said, 'You would love the shop. It's really great, as they support the local community with their dairy products, from their own pedigree Guernsey cows. They sell milk, yoghurt, cheese, cream and even have their own butter!'

Nannie turned around in her seat to look at Mum and said, 'I'd love to go there sometime.'

Jack said, 'Mum, can we take Nannie and Grandpops to the café for something to eat later on?'

'I can't see why not?' Mum said smiling at him as he nodded excitedly.

'We'll see,' Dad said interrupting Mum, as he looked at them in the rear view mirror.

Blue saw the disappointment on both Jack's and Mum's faces.

'It would be great to take Mum and Dad there, especially, if the weather stays bright and sunny, we could always come back this way and have tea there tonight. They only open in the evening on a Friday and Saturday night,' she explained.

'Let's just wait and see,' Dad said sternly.

Blue wondered what the matter was with Dad. He wasn't his normal happy self. Something seemed to be bothering him. Blue wanted to know if there was something he could do to make Dad smile again. He hoped and wished that by the end of the day, Dad would have a smile on his face.

Shortly afterwards, they arrived at Havenstreet and made their way to the booth to hand in their ticket.

'Hello there, how can I help you?' said a lady, whose name badge read 'Liz Smith'.

Jack had persuaded his mum to let him hold the ticket, so he pushed it towards her.

'We won the Easter egg competition at the Botanical Gardens last week, for us all to go on the steam train. Me and Blue, my bear can't wait to go on it.' He beamed at her.

'Congratulations on winning the golden ticket,' she said as she tore the strip off the side of it, handing it back to him.

They moved out of the way to let Nannie and Grandpops pay for their tickets.

Mum turned to the boys.

'Right, what do you want to do first?' She asked looking at their excited faces.

'We would like to go on the steam train, wouldn't we, Tom?' Jack said hugging Blue.

'Well how about we go on the train first, and then we

can come back and look around in the museum they have here,' Mum said as everyone nodded.

They heard the train blowing its whistle as it thundered into the station. The gate to the platform had been shut to allow the train to pull in. Once it stopped, the gate was opened for the passengers to allow them onto the platform and to board the train.

'All aboard!' The guard shouted, making sure that everyone got inside the carriages and shut the door behind them, before he blew his whistle, letting the driver know it was safe for him to pull away. They all got into the nearest carriage and settled down, ready for the ride.

'I think the train will go to Wootton first, before the steam engine gets removed and taken to the back of the train to pull it back again. It will go through here and take us to Smallbrook, before finally coming back here again,' Mum said smiling at everyone.

'Dad, can I stand up and look out of the window?' Jack asked, going to stand.

'No… sit down,' Dad said sternly.

'But, I…I only wanted to show Blue?' Jack mumbled biting his lip.

'I'm sure your Dad didn't mean to shout at you. All he meant was that it's dangerous for you to open the window and look out, especially when we are moving. Look, there's a sign above the window, which says you are not allowed to do it,' Nannie said smiling at him.

However, Jack was upset and no words of comfort helped as he held Blue tightly in his arms. Nannie moved closer to him and put her arm around his shoulders.

The train started gathering speed, making its way to Wootton. When they got there, the train stopped and the engine was removed from the front of the train and attached to the back of it. Jack's face lit up, when he saw the engine go past the carriage.

'Did you see that Blue? All the coal the men have to put into the fire to make the train go faster,' Jack said looking at him.

'Perhaps when we get back to the station, we can go and look at the engine and speak to the driver,' Grandpops said, smiling at both Tom and Jack.

'That would be cool, Grandpops,' Tom said looking at Jack who nodded at him.

When the train pulled into the station again, Mum and Nannie decided they would take advantage of the café there and have a quick cup of tea, while Grandpops and the boys went to speak to the driver.

'Are you going with Grandpops and the boys or coming with Nannie and me for a cup of tea?' Mum asked Dad.

'No, I think I'll have a walk around. I've been thinking about something on the train journey,' Dad said.

'Okay. Will you and the boys be alright, Grandpops?' Mum asked.

'Yes, you and Nannie go and have a quick cuppa, and once, the boys and I have checked out the engine, we'll come and find you. Then we can go and have a look in the museum,' Grandpops said, taking both boys by the hand.

Everyone went in different directions. Mum and Nannie to the café, and Dad strolled off to another part of the station, as Grandpops took the boys to look at the engine.

When they got there the driver was busy wiping his brow with his handkerchief.

'That must be hard work driving the train,' Jack said to him.

'Yes, it is, but it's also a lot of fun too,' he said smiling at him. 'I'm a volunteer here at the railway. My wife works here too. She was on the counter today; I expect she sold you your tickets.'

'No, we won our ticket with the Easter egg hunt competition,' Jack said.

'That's wonderful. Did you enjoy your ride on the train?'

Both boys nodded their heads.

'We loved it when the engine moved to the back and we got to see it, didn't we Jack?' Tom said.

The man nodded.

'Would you like to come aboard and I can show you how the engine works?'

'Would we?' Grandpops said as he and the boys stepped aboard.

It was slightly crowded in the engine, but they stood close together where they got to see exactly what the driver and his co-driver did. They saw the coal and the man, whose name was Chris, opened the fire hole to show them where it went. He also showed them all the different switches and most importantly of all, the brake.

It was all so interesting, and they were fascinated with everything Chris had to tell them.

'I wish I could drive the train,' Jack eventually said when Chris had finished talking.

Chris smiled at him.

'Perhaps when you're a bit older. And then you could volunteer like me. I've always loved steam trains.'

'Cor, that would be brilliant, wouldn't it Tom, to drive a real steam train?' Jack said, completely taken with the idea.

'Well, I think it's time we thanked Chris for being so

kind in showing us the engine. I expect your Mum, Nan and Dad will be wondering where we've got to.'

'Thank you, Chris,' the boys chorused as they got down from the engine.

Taking hold of their Grandpops hands again, they went to find their Mum and Nan in the café.

'That was perfect timing,' Nannie said as she saw them.

'Did you have a good time?' Mum asked.

'Did we ever,' Grandpops said, telling them all about it.

When he finished, Mum looked past him.

'Have you seen your Dad?' she asked the boys.

'No, we haven't. We thought he'd be here with you,' Grandpops said.

'Mum, why is Dad grumpy?' Jack asked.

Blue looked at Mum, as he too was anxious to know just why Dad was sad.

Mum looked a bit embarrassed, her face went slightly red.

'Dad hasn't had much work on lately, and, he's been worried about it. He didn't mean to snap at you,' she said looking at Jack, as she bit her lip. Dad's worried about money, and if we will have enough to tide us over until his other jobs start picking up, which I'm sure they will do, especially now as the good weather's on its way.'

Jack looked at Blue and hugged his pal to him.

Just then, Jack turned around and saw his Dad striding over to where they were. He was smiling broadly at them all.

'Hey you guys, I've been looking for you. I've got the best news ever!'

Everyone turned towards him, wanting to hear his

news. Blue was all ears too.

'You'll never believe it?' Dad said excitedly. 'As I was wondering around the station I bumped into a lady that I went and saw last year about re-designing her garden, Isobel Russell. Unfortunately, she had to leave the island for a while. But now she's back for good and is eager for me to make a start on it as soon as possible.'

'Oh, that's wonderful,' Mum said going forwards and pulling him close to her and kissing him on the lips.

'Yuck!' Jack shouted out, shielding Blue's eyes.

'That's brilliant news, and cause for celebration. What do you say, we have a look around the museum, and then afterwards, we go to Bluebell's café for our tea. It will be our treat!' Nannie said smiling at Mum and Dad.

'Yes, your Nannie's right. It will be our way of saying thank you, for having us to stay with you,' Grandpops said.

'Yippee,' Jack said dancing around.

'We're going to the farm to see the calves again Blue.'

Blue could see that Dad was smiling again, and was pleased that, at the end of the day, he had got his wish and everyone was happy.

10
BLUE'S MURDER MYSTERY ADVENTURE

'Mum can we have some sweets?' Jack asked one day when they were in the Post Office.

'Only something little, I don't want you ruining your appetite, before tea,' Mum said.

'Well in that case then, we have some penny sweets here, what about having some of those?' Vince, who was serving them, said.

The boys nodded.

'How much are you allowed?' Vince asked.

Mum overhearing said, 'They can have fifteen pence worth each. They don't normally have sweets in the week, but they did very well at school today. They got certificates, so I'm making an exception,' she said smiling at the boys.

'Oh, have you seen the posters about what the village is doing during The Crime Festival season?' Jacqui said. 'Because local crime authors Carol and Bob Bridgestock are doing a book signing in the village at half term, we have decided with a few of the other local businesses here to have a murder mystery day, with a bit of a difference.'

'That sounds like really good fun, but what about the children?' Mum said.

'We thought we would have a Cluedo sort of game for the children.'

'Yes, and Tom, Blue and me would love to be detectives and solve a murder,' Jack said overhearing the conversation.

'All the money from the event will all go to the charity that we are supporting here at the Post Office, Age UK along with Island Community Ventures.'

'That's a great charity,' Mum agreed. 'What day is it going to be?'

'The children's murder mystery is on the Friday from noon onwards. We will have clues at various locations in the village for the children to try to figure out who the murderer is, where they did it and just how they did it.'

'Please, Mum, can we have a go?' Tom asked.

'How will we know where to look?' Jack asked

'What we are going to do is sell leaflets and on that leaflet, is the first clue on where to go in the village to find one of the characters we've made up. When you find that character, along with a weapon, you can cross that off your list, and then you will be given a clue to the next location, and it will carry on like that until you have two possibilities left.'

'That sounds like fun, Blue, doesn't it?' Jack said.

Jacqui smiled and said, 'We will have characters, similar to Cluedo characters. Our, would be murderers, are called, Mr Ray Sunshine, Miss Candy Floss, Mrs C Green, Mrs Skye Blue, Mr Grey Granite, and lastly Dr Tango. These people are going to be at various places in the village, and you have to solve the clues to see where they are, and work out at the end who committed the murder, where they did it, and what the murder weapon was. There are going to be two possible stories, and at the end of the day, all the right guesses will be put into a box and a winner will be drawn out.'

Jack, hearing this, said, 'Do you know what the prize will be?'

'Yes, it's going to be a great prize. But, I'm keeping it secret until the day,' Jacqui said tapping the side of her nose with her finger.

'Oh,' Jack said as he turned to Blue. 'That sounds like good fun, I can't wait, Can you, Blue? I think me and Blue will make great detectives. Mum, do we have a magnifying glass at home that we can use to hunt for clues?'

'Well you'll have a couple of weeks to hone up on your detecting skills,' Vince said overhearing what Jack had said, before winking at him and Blue.

'Half term can't come soon enough now,' Jack said to Blue and Tom.

'And we'll tell the other school children about it too!' Mum said nodding at Jacqui.

'I wonder if Taz and the others will join in,' Jack said.

'I think that Taz is off to the mainland again to see his mum for the week. But, you can ask him,' Mum said.

'Yes, it will be good fun,' Tom agreed.

Soon, it was half term week, and Jack was disappointed, that Taz was going away. He would have lots to tell Taz, when he came home.

During half term, when Mum and Dad had to go to work, Sam Farren came over and looked after the boys, until Mum came home. One day when Mum and Dad had gone, Sam turned to the boys.

'Right, what do you want to do?'

'Mum, found her old game of Cluedo, do you think we can play it? That way we will know how to look for clues for real on Friday,' Tom said.

'I can't see why not. Let's go and set it up on the table,' Sam said leading the way.

After a fun filled morning playing the game, which

Tom won, much to Jack's disgust, both boys went and played outside with their football. Soon Mum was home, she had a carrier bag with her.

'Hi boys, have you been good for Sam?'

'They've been great, and are very good detectives too,' Sam said smiling and winking at them.

'That's good to hear, and I have a surprise for you both,' Mum said lifting out of the bag, two children's police helmets.

'Wow! They're great, Mum,' Jack said going forwards to her as she placed a helmet on his head.

'Here you go, Tom, this one's for you, it's an inspectors hat, I was talking to Betty Jordan at work, and she said she had some old dressing up clothes at home, that her children no longer want, and would I like them for you? I've also got some policemen's outfits to go with the hats,' Mum said smiling at their eager faces.

Tom took the inspectors hat and put it on his head, as he and Jack looked at themselves in the hall mirror.

'We look like real policemen,' Jack jumped up and down, but then stopped.

'What about Blue? We haven't got anything for Blue to wear.'

'Well, actually, I have a little something that I have been working on for Blue,' Mum said going upstairs to her bedroom.

A couple of minutes later she came back down with another carrier bag.

'Here you go,' she said turning to Jack and handing him the bag.

Jack put his hand into the bag and pulled out a hat. But, it was a strange looking hat.

'Try putting it on Blue's head,' Mum said, as Jack

reluctantly pulled his pal over towards him, pulling the hat down on his head.

'He looks silly!' Jack said.

Mum's face fell, but Sam quickly chipped in.

'Do you know that all the best detectives wear hats like that? It's called a deerstalker, and there's a famous detective called Sherlock Holmes who always wore one. Why he couldn't detect a crime without it.'

Jack turned to Sam.

'Really, is that true?'

Sam nodded. 'I tell you what, why don't I Google a picture of him for you to see, okay?'

Jack brightened up. 'Thanks, Mum,' he said giving her a hug.

'You're welcome. And when you and Tom wear the helmets on Friday, Bob Bridgestock will be there, and you can show him your hats, as he was a real life detective, before he retired.'

'Cor, I'll get to meet a real life policeman,' Jack said.

The rest of the week went very quickly, and on Friday the boys put on their detective outfits, along with the helmets. Blue had his deerstalker on his head, and looked the part of a great detective. Jack had been convinced after seeing pictures on the internet of Sherlock Holmes. With his magnifying glass at hand, he and Blue were ready to track any clues they might find to lead them to their murderer.

In the Post Office they bought copies of the leaflet with the first clue on it.

'Good luck, boys,' Jacqui and Vince said as they went back outside.

'Right, let me read this out,' Mum said.

"A murder has been committed, we don't know who

did it, or where, or with what. All we know, is you have six suspects, six rooms and six murder weapons to choose from.

The six suspects are: Mr Ray Sunshine, Miss Candy Floss, Mrs C Green, Mrs Skye Blue, Mr Grey Granite and Dr Tango.

The six rooms that the murder could have been committed in are: The Library, The Kitchen, The Cellar, The Conservatory, The Hall and The Dining Room."

Mum looked at the boys.

'Are you ready, for your first clue?' she said. Jack and Tom nodded.

'"You will find me if you like to go into gardens, I am in the middle of something; you have to go up and down?"'

'Oh, I know where that is?' Jack said jumping up and down with Blue in his arms. 'It's got to be the Model Village. Come on?' He said dragging his mum by the arm and pulling her towards the Model Village.

However, when they got to the entrance, there was a sign outside, saying the Model Village wasn't taking part in the competition. But they wished those who were the very best of luck.

'You're wrong,' Tom said shaking his head as he looked at Mum. 'Can you read the clue again, please?'

Mum did as she was asked, and whilst they were standing there, a couple more murder hunters joined them. It was getting exciting, all of them trying to work out the clue.

Mum bent down and whispered to the boys.

'Do you think they mean the Griffin pub? In their garden they have a maze, and it does say here in the clue, I am in the middle of something; you have to go up and down.'

'Yes, Blue and I think you're right,' Jack said urging his mum and Tom towards the Griffin.

In the garden, there was the maze. It was tricky trying to work out which way to go, and several times they took the wrong turning. Eventually, they made it to the middle.

'Look, Blue, we've found one of the characters,' Jack said hugging Blue to him as they rushed over to where Mr Ray Sunshine was sitting.

'Congratulations,' he said as they got to him. 'Now have a look around and see what I have with me. There are clues to what room is represented here and what weapon you can see too. And then you can cross me off your list.' He smiled at them as the boys took in everything that was there.

'Have you got clue number two?' Mum asked, as Mr Sunshine nodded and handed her a piece of paper.

'Look, Tom there are some books here, what are the rooms on the leaflet?'

'The Library, I think this is supposed to be that room. And look Jack; can you see the rope by Mr Sunshine's legs?'

Jack nodded and crossed Mr Sunshine, The Library and The Rope off his list.

'Right, shall we get onto clue number two?' Mum said, as the boys nodded.

"I'm easy to find, you can sit inside me, but then again are you on the outside of me?"

'I know where that is, I think it's The Hollies, because they have a conservatory,' Tom said, but then Jack interrupted him.

'But, doesn't the Old Smithy have one too?'

'Your brother's right, Tom,' Mum said. 'How about we

go to the Old Smithy first, and if the second clue isn't there, we go on to The Hollies?'

Both boys nodded, as they turned around and made their way out of the maze again. They were met by some other people going in and smiled at them. Crossing the road, they made their way to the Old Smithy, going into the conservatory, but there was nobody and nothing there. So they left there and went to The Hollies.

However, by this time, they weren't the first ones there.

'We should have come here first,' Tom shouted at Mum and Jack.

'It's only a game, and at the end of the day, it's the taking part, Tom. It doesn't matter who gets here first anyway. We have to pick the right murderer, weapon and place where it happened.'

Tom looked down at the ground, before muttering, 'Sorry.'

They went into the conservatory and sitting there was a lady dressed in a pink fluffy dress, with a pink fluffy wig on her head.

'Mrs Candyfloss,' Jack said to Blue, as he crossed her out on the list, along with the conservatory.

They had to look pretty hard to find a weapon. At first no one noticed it, because it was sitting on top of the piano, and everyone thought it was supposed to be there. It was only when Mum eventually saw it, that she realised the candlestick was the other weapon to be crossed off the list.

Mrs Candyfloss gave them their third clue and coming out of the conservatory, Mum read it out.

"You will find me where there's sweet food galore!"

Mum shouted it out in full hearing of everyone else,

still on the murder hunt, 'It's Chocolate Island.'

'Shush, Mum!' the boys shouted at her.

'Oops, sorry,' she said as they and the others on the hunt all rushed up the road to the chocolate shop.

Bursting through the front door of the shop, they rushed to the back where the ladies who worked there were busy making some chocolates. Jack was totally enthralled, when he saw them tipping chocolates out of the plastic moulds. Once the chocolates cooled down, each chocolate was hand painted with, milk, dark or white chocolate.

Mum laughed, as Jack ran his tongue over his lips.

'Mum, look,' shouted Tom, as he pointed at another character, who was on their list.

It was Dr Tango. The man was dressed in a bright orange suit and holding a medical bag. As much as they tried, no one could find the weapon. They all walked up to him, and Tom even undid the medical bag, but there wasn't anything inside it.

Dr Tango was standing by some chocolates, which he was cutting up and giving the pieces to the children.

Blue could see immediately what the weapon was; it was the knife the doctor was using. Jack walked forward to get a piece of chocolate from the tray the doctor was holding, and just as he went to get a piece, Blue jumped and dropped on top of the chocolate.

'Sorry,' Jack said going to pick up Blue.

However, as he took hold of Blue, he grabbed the knife too. His face said it all, when he realised what was in his hand.

'Clever, Blue, you found the weapon,' he said hugging his pal close to him, before crossing The Knife off the list.

Putting the knife back on the tray, he turned towards

his mum, who was holding the fourth and final clue in her hands.

'Come on boys, let's go outside and I'll read it out to you.

'"Fruits galore is one of the clues you have to find me. You might have to go deep down into the ground too!"'

That seemed to have them all stumped.

'Where's that then, Mum?' Jack said scratching his head.

'I'm not too sure? The Old Smithy does have a stall where they sell raspberries, but I didn't see it after we came out of the conservatory there. Look, why don't we just walk down the road and see if anything looks like it might have fruit in it?'

The boys nodded, and they set off back down into the village. They walked past the Post Office, and Jacqui stuck her head out of the door.

'How's it all going?'

'We're on the fourth and final clue, but we're a bit stuck,' Tom said.

'Well, you're doing really well. I'm sure you'll figure out that last clue,' Jacqui said smiling at them as they carried on their way.

They went past The Hollies getting to the memorial bench by the bus stop. Mum sat down on it, with the boys sitting either side of her.

'If we carry on down this way, what shops are we going to pass?' Tom said.

'Well on the other side of the road is the model toy shop, and The Old World Tea Gardens, and the Griffin, but the clue won't be at the Griffin again. And on this side, there's the sweet shop and Godshill Cider, and round the corner…' Mum stopped speaking, 'I think I've got it. Come on boys,' she said giggling.

Jack looked up the road to see some of the other murder mystery hunters scratching their heads.

'What, Mum, where is it?'

'Follow me.'

They made their way to the building where Mum was convinced the fourth clue was to be found. Godshill Cider!

'You're right,' Jack shouted out as he ran inside and saw someone dressed completely in green.

'Mrs C Green,' Tom said looking at her and leaning over to the pad Jack held, he crossed off her name and the location.

It was obvious it was meant to be the cellar. Now where was the weapon? Suddenly, Jack spied an old beer barrel and on top of it was a wrench. He crossed that out too. Now they had to make their minds up between the murderer being Mrs Skye Blue or Mr Grey Granite. And did they commit the murder in the dining room or the hall, with either the lead-pipe or the gun?

Mum walked over to Mrs C Green, and she gave her a piece of paper with yet another clue. They all went back outside and walked back to the bench by the bus stop to try to work out, who, where and what.

'"Congratulations on getting this far, now who is the murderer? A couple of clues for you to work it out, this person can be seen in the sky. They love this room, when they come into the house. And what tool could they use?"'

Mum read it out and said, 'That's not really very helpful. This person can be seen in the sky; well you get blue sky and grey skies. They love this room. In lots of houses the first room you walk into is the kitchen, but then again, the first room could be the hall. And what tool could they use? What do you use a lead-pipe for now, and a gun? No-one has a gun, unless they have a shotgun for clay pigeon shooting,' she shook her head.

'What do you think we should do?' Jack said, as he held Blue close.

'I think that each of you should write down who YOU think the murderer is, where they did it and with what. And then we should put your answers in for the draw and hope for the best.'

The boys nodded, and Mum gave them their entry forms to fill in. Jack was whispering to Blue and nodding his head, as he filled in the form. Afterwards they took them back to the Post Office where they put them into a box Jacqui had behind the counter. Jack crossed his fingers.

At six o'clock, everyone gathered in The Essex for the results of the murder mystery. The guests of honour were Carol and Bob Bridgestock. Everyone was talking, saying what a good idea the murder mystery had been. And what a lot of fun it was too. When the box was brought out, all went quiet.

Bob Bridgestock stood up.

'I think that's my cue to speak and put you all out of your misery,' he said as everyone laughed.

'First off, I have to thank everyone here in Godshill who has taken part in this children's murder mystery. The Post Office, Chocolate Island, The Griffin, The Hollies and Godshill Cider. Jacqui has told me that the money raised from today's mystery is nearly £150 pounds. Well done everyone, give yourselves a round of applause,' Bob said looking round the room as everyone clapped and cheered.

'Right, now for the bit you've been waiting for. Those of you, who put your entry slips in, I have to let you know that every single entry was sifted through to see who had given the correct answers. We only had eight people give the right answers. But, before, I ask my wife, to choose a winner; I have to let you know it wasn't Mrs Skye Blue, with the lead-pipe in the hall. So I think that gives the game away.'

There were murmurings of, 'I told you so.'

At that, everyone laughed.

'Just in case you didn't work out who the murder was, and in which room it took part, and with what weapon, I will now tell you. It was Mr Grey Granite, in the hall with the gun!'

Again there were murmurings of, 'I told you so.'

To which everyone laughed again.

'And now, without further ado, I would like my wife to come over here and pick a winner out of the box.'

With that, Carol stood up and walked over putting her hand into the box, pulling out an entry form. She opened it up and looked at it quizzically.

'The winner of the murder mystery competition is…Blue the bear.'

'Jack!' Mum said, as everyone turned and looked at him as he stood up clutching Blue in his arms.

'Well as Blue found the knife for the third clue, I thought it only right that I put his name on the entry form.'

'Many congratulations to you then, Blue?' Carol said shaking his paw when Jack took him over to her.

She handed Jack an envelope.

This is Blue's prize, which I'm sure he won't mind sharing with you. It's a trip to Newport Police Station, to have a look around there, and to go down to the cells, and the best bit is you get to have a ride in a police car. And, not only that, but The Essex here, has also thrown in an extra prize of afternoon tea for four.'

Jack looked at Mum and Tom and smiled at them.

'Well I think we should give Blue and Jack a round of applause, don't you?' said Bob as he clapped Jack who walked back to his seat where Mum stood up and gave him a big hug.

'It looks like you made the right hat for Blue after all, Mum,' Jack said. 'He made a great detective, didn't you, Blue?'

Blue was very happy and besides how could someone with the name Mrs Skye Blue have killed anyone? Blue was a good name.

11
BLUE'S BIRTHDAY PARTY ADVENTURE

Jack took Blue into Mum and Dad's bedroom. Blue looked over at Rose who was still perched on top of the chest of drawers. He smiled at her as she winked back at him. Jack jumped onto Mum's bed and he too looked over at Rose.

'Why can't me and Blue play with Rose?'

'Because, she's not a toy,' Mum said.

Jack was puzzled.

'I mean, of course she's a toy, but not one I want anyone playing with. To me, she's a very special teddy bear, and I'm so lucky that your Dad bought her for me. However, I have to be careful with her, because she was so very expensive.'

'That's sad for Rose though as she doesn't have any adventures. Can't I play with her, with Blue?'

'No, sweetheart, I'm afraid not. Rose is just going to be a look at bear, not a play and touch one.'

Jack's wasn't very happy, but if that's what Mum said, then he knew he would have to listen to her. After all, Rose was her bear!

Blue on hearing this bit of news was sad too. He was hoping that he and Rose could have had many a happy play time together. Now it seemed they couldn't. What was he going to do?

Rose gave Blue a gloomy look too.

'I think this is where she's going to stay from now on,' Mum said, getting up and placing Rose as far back as she could on her chest of drawers.

Jack looked at her and nodded, as he went out of the room, taking Blue with him.

Over the next couple of days, whenever Jack took Blue into Mum and Dad's bedroom, they always saw Rose, still in the same place, stuck on top of the chest of drawers, out of reach of anyone. Blue couldn't stop thinking about Rose. There just had to be a way of talking to her!

Once he'd tried when Jack was fast asleep in bed. He crept out of the bedroom and went along the landing, but he'd been unsuccessful.

'What on earth are you doing here?' Mum had said as she came to check on the boys.

Picking Blue up, she'd taken him back into Jack's room, putting Blue underneath Jack's arm, so he couldn't move. There just had to be another way of seeing Rose, Blue thought sadly.

When Jack woke the next morning, he was excited. 'It's not long until it's my birthday. It's only two weeks away, and I can't wait, although I'm not as old as you, pal,' he said looking at Blue and shaking his head as he laughed.

Recently, Jack and Mum had googled Blue on the internet. They thought he was almost one hundred years old.

Mum was constantly asking Jack what he wanted for his birthday. The last time she asked, Jack told her he didn't know what he wanted.

'No, I don't know. The only thing I ever wanted was a puppy and a teddy bear. And now I've got Blue. So that just leaves a puppy,' he said looking at Mum and smiling.

At that Mum shook her head.

'Think again, we're not having a puppy.'

'Why?' Tom and Jack both asked.

'Because, Dad and I are at work during the week, and there wouldn't be anyone here to look after it. It wouldn't be fair,' Mum replied. Changing the subject quickly, she said, 'Well how about a party? Do you want a themed one, like Cowboys and Indians, Spacemen, Superheroes?'

Again, Jack just shrugged his shoulders and shook his head.

Blue had never celebrated his birthday, and had never been to a party before. Would it be exciting? He wondered.

'How about Space Island or Jungle Jim's Adventure play ground?' Tom asked.

'No, Adam had his party at Jungle Jim's; I don't want to have the same as him.'

'Well have a think and think fast if we're going to send invitations out to all your friends soon,' Mum said.

'I will,' Jack said hugging Blue as he whispered to him, 'Help me think of something that I want for my birthday, and help me think of what party I should have.'

Blue wanted to help his pal out, but wasn't sure he could. Perhaps Rose could help him think of something. He would have to try and speak to her somehow.

That night when Jack was fast asleep in bed, and Blue heard Mum and Dad in the lounge listening to the television, he made up his mind, tonight was the night he was going to find his friend Rose and talk to her.

Creeping along the landing, Blue breathed a sigh of relief as he made it to the stairs leading to Mum and Dad's bedroom where Rose was. Blue was mightily glad there were only the three steps, as he huffed and puffed, pulling himself up them. At the top, he ran to the door and looked in. There was Rose, still perched up on Mum's chest of drawers.

'Blue! What are you doing here?' Rose called out, as she saw Blue run over to her.

'Can you get down from there?' He shouted up, as Rose walked to the edge of the drawers.

Sitting down, she swung herself off, landing on top of the laundry basket.

'It's wonderful to see you?' She smiled at him.

Blue shyly nodded, suddenly, he was lost for words. However, he knew he would have to speak soon, because if Mum came into the room, then his getting to see Rose would have been in vain.

'I need to ask you something?' he finally blurted out.

'What is it?' Rose asked.

Blue explained all about how it was Jack's birthday in a couple of weeks, and the fact that Jack didn't know what he wanted for a present, or what sort of party he wanted to have either. Blue told Rose about how Jack had wanted a puppy, but Mum had said no!

Rose listened to all he had to say, and she scratched her head.

'Leave it with me and I'll think about it. I'm sure that between the two of us, we can come up with something.' Rose smiled at Blue. 'It's so good to see and speak to you. I've really missed you,' Rose said glumly.

Blue nodded.

'Me too, it's horrible that we can't play together. I wish we could find a way that we could,' Blue replied.

Just then before Rose could say anything else, the light in the bedroom was turned on.

'What on earth are you doing here?' Mum said bending down and picking up Blue. She then noticed Rose sitting on top of the laundry basket. 'And what are you doing there?' Mum picked up Rose and put her back on top of the chest of drawers as she shook her head.

Dad came into the bedroom.

'What's Blue doing in here?' Dad said coming up behind Mum.

'Jack must have crept in here to see Rose,' Mum replied. 'I'm going to have to have a word with him. I thought I'd already told him, that Rose is not a bear I want anyone playing with.'

Suddenly, Blue felt bad. Had he got Jack into trouble?

'Don't be too hard with him. He's only young and I know you told him not to play with her, but I'm sure he wouldn't do anything to harm your bear, look how he looks after Blue,' Dad said putting his arm around Mum.

Mum gave Dad a brief smile. 'I'll just take Blue back to Jack. It's odd he didn't take him when he went back to his room,' Mum said as she walked out of the bedroom, carrying Blue in her arms.

Rose gave Blue a sly wink, which no one saw.

The next day, Mum asked Jack if he had been in her room the previous evening and had he touched Rose?

'No,' Jack said looking puzzled as Blue looked on anxious.

'Okay,' Mum said, as Blue breathed a huge sigh of relief. Then changing the subject she said, 'I've had an idea I wanted to run past you about your party.'

Jack looked up at her. 'What idea?'

'Well you know the other week when we found out that Blue was probably around one hundred years old?'

Jack nodded.

'Something came to me in the night, and I've been thinking, what if we had a joint birthday for you and Blue? We could have a teddy bear's picnic theme party, celebrating your birthday and Blue's special centenary birthday.'

'What's centenary mean?' Jack asked.

'It's a word meaning one hundred, and in this case we would be celebrating one hundred years since we think Blue was made, so we could say it was his birthday too.' Mum smiled at Jack. 'What do you and Blue think about that?'

Jack looked at Blue and smiled, before saying, 'It's a great idea. All my friends could bring their favourite toys to the party, and we could have a toy party for them, and you could bring Rose to the party.'

'That's funny you should say that,' Mum said, 'Because there was something telling me that I should have my bear come to your party too! So that's your party decided, all we have to think about now, is a gift for you.'

Jack nodded looking at Blue and smiling.

'What do you think of that pal? A teddy bear picnic party and we get to have Rose come to it.'

Blue was so happy, he thought he would burst.

'So have you given anymore thought about what Dad and I can get you as a gift?' Mum said.

'Well, I do like Lego and it would be great to have a trampoline outside to jump on.'

Mum raised her eyebrows.

'Well, at least that gives me something to go on,' Mum said looking relieved. 'Do you want to help me make up some invitations for your party? And then we can write them out, and you can give them to your friends on Monday,' Mum said walking over to the computer and switching it on.

Once the invitations were made and written out, Jack put them in his bag ready to hand out to all his friends at school.

'I can't wait to come to your party?' Taz said, 'And I'm going to bring Tiger.

'Yes, I'm going to bring my Lucy doll,' Charlotte said.

The children's cheerful chatter, discussing what they were going to bring to the party, made Blue just as happy as it did Jack. He couldn't wait for Jack's birthday and the party, because Rose was coming too!

A week later it was the big day, but unfortunately for Jack, it was a school day too. After opening all his cards, Jack started on his presents.

'Here you go, Jack,' Tom said handing his little brother a wrapped box.

'Cor, thanks, Tom,' Jack's face lit up as he eagerly ripped the paper away to reveal an action man.

Then Mum handed Jack a few presents.

'There's one from Nanny and Grandpops for you,' Mum said.

'Thanks, Mum for my presents,' Jack said looking at the three boxes of Lego toys, that he'd unwrapped.

'You are very welcome, but don't forget, they weren't all from me and Dad. You will have to send Nanny and Grandpops a thank you note, but, for now, it's time for you both to get ready for school.'

'Mum, hasn't Blue got any presents to undo?' Jack said looking around. 'It is his birthday too!'

'Yes, I've got something for Blue, but he will have to have it later,' Mum said.

The school day went very quickly, and before long Mum was collecting both boys from school. The party was due to start soon.

'Mum, have you got Blue's present?' Jack asked.

'I have, but he's going to have to wait until later, when Dad gets home.'

'Oh, okay,' Jack said forlornly.

Just then the doorbell rang and Jack rushed to open the door to let his friends in. Everyone brought presents for Jack and some brought presents for Blue too. Molly's Nan had made Blue a shirt and shorts, for the summer. And the twins had got him a sun hat and sun glasses. Jack helped Blue open his presents.

Then they played a couple of party games, pass the parcel and musical statues, before it was time for the Teddy Bear's Picnic. A small table was set up for all of the toys to sit around.

When Mum brought Rose downstairs and to the table, Blue's eyes lit up, especially when Rose was placed next to him. There were plastic plates and tea cups, also plastic knives and forks set on the table. Tom had brought out all the plastic food that he had too. So it looked like Blue had his own birthday food including a birthday cake.

'What a wonderful party,' Rose whispered to Blue.

'Yes, it is. And I don't think it would have happened without you. How did you get Mum to think of having this sort of party?' Blue asked her.

'Well, when Mum was in her bedroom one time, she had her television on and they were talking about nursery rhymes for children, when they mentioned, "the teddy bears picnic" I thought what a great idea for a party, so when Mum went to sleep that night, I climbed down and whispered in her ear, about having a themed teddy bears picnic party.' Rose smiled at Blue.

'Well, I'm so happy you did,' Blue whispered back. 'Did you give her any idea as to what to get Jack for his birthday present?'

'You will just have to wait and see,' Rose said winking at him.

'But, hasn't Jack had all his presents from Mum and Dad?'

Rose put her paw to her mouth. Now Blue was puzzled.

Jack and his friends enjoyed their birthday tea. Mum made lots of savoury food, including sandwiches, sausage rolls and crisps. She also had an assortment of sweet food, like cakes and biscuits. Jack's eyes lit up at the birthday cake when Mum brought it into the room.

'Right, are we all going to sing Happy Birthday?'

At that, everyone joined in with singing to not just Jack, but to Blue too. Afterwards, Jack picked Blue up and together, they blew out the candles.

'I only put a few candles on the cake, because I didn't think there would be enough room to put all one hundred on it,' Mum said smiling happily at Jack and Blue.

'Oh wow, look at the cake,' Jack said excitedly pointing at it.

Mum had made it in the shape of a teddy bear, someone who Jack, instantly recognised, once the candles were blown out.

'Look, everyone, it's Blue.'

'Okay, who wants a piece?' Mum asked putting the cake down on the table and cutting it up. Everyone put their hands up, shouting out, 'Me, me!'

After they had all had enough food, Mum suggested the children went and played outside in the garden. Luckily, a couple of the parents had come with their children, and were able to organise games outside, whilst Mum and Taz's Nan, cleared up the tables.

All the toys were put onto the mantelpiece, where they could see out into the garden, and watch the children having fun there. All too soon, it was time for everyone to go home.

'We've had such a great time,' Molly said waving goodbye as she and the others all went out of the front door taking their toys with them.

When they'd all gone, Mum went into the kitchen to make herself a cup of tea. Jack picked up Blue from the mantelpiece and was playing with him, when she came back in.

'Mum, I thought you said you were going to get Blue a birthday present?' Jack asked.

'Well…' before she could say anymore, Dad walked in through the door.

'Cor, is there a cuppa going for me?' he said spotting Mum's cup of tea.

'Yes, I'll just go and make you one,' she said rushing from the room.

Dad walked further into the room with a great big smile on his face.

'Dad, you missed my party,' Jack said going up to him and giving him a hug.

'I know, son, and I'm really sorry, but there was someone I had to collect,' he said winking at Mum as she walked back in.

Blue looked at Rose on the mantelpiece as she winked back at him.

'Can everyone sit down for a minute, because the 'someone,' I had to get might get very excited, when he sees you.'

At that, Tom and Jack sat down on the floor, whilst Mum put hers and Dad's cups of tea on the table. Dad went back outside and when he came in next he was carrying a black and tan puppy in his arms.

Jack and Tom looked at one another before shouting

out, 'It's a puppy!' and rushed over to their Dad.

Dad put the puppy on the floor, and immediately he went over to the boys who made a great fuss of him. They were gently stroking him and tickling his tummy.

'He's lovely, Dad. What's he called?' Tom asked.

'Well the ladies at the RSPCA centre said his name is Jet. They said as he is so young, he might get used to another name, that's if you don't like the one he has,' Dad said.

Suddenly, Jet ran round and round the room. He was running from one person to another.

'Do you know what, Dad; I think his name suits him, don't you, Jack?' Tom said smiling at the puppy's antics as Jack nodded.

'What sort of dog is he?' Jack asked stroking the puppy on its head.

'He's an unusual breed; he's called a Lancashire Heeler. Jet was owned by a lady who had to give him up, as she became allergic to his fur, not long after getting him. She recently moved to the island from the mainland, and so was unable to return him to his breeder. So when Mum and I went to the RSPCA, the ladies there thought we would be ideal people to own him,' Dad said smiling at the boys with Jet.

Mum came up to them and said, 'He's for all the family. We shall each take turns walking him, and feeding him, and clearing up after him too!' Tom scrunched his nose up.

'Mum, I thought you said we couldn't have a puppy?' Jack said tickling Jet on his belly as he rolled over.

Mum nodded and said, 'I know I did. But, when Dad and I discussed having a dog, and the fact it would be left at home when we were at work, Dad said there was no reason for that to happen. He can take the dog to work with him. And, because Jet is that bit older, even though he's still a puppy, he's already had all of his inoculations. That means, he can start going to work with your Dad straight away once his work picks up. In the meantime, we can all work at training Jet, to sit and stay, and fetch.'

'He'll be just the right sized dog to come out and about with me, on any gardening jobs I do,' Dad said laughing at Jet's antics.

Just then Jet spied Blue, making a bee line for him. He grabbed hold of Blue in his mouth and started shaking his leg. Dad was quick to gently prise Jet's mouth open and retrieve Blue.

Blue was very glad that Dad had got to him as quickly as he did. Jet's teeth were biting his fur.

'You boys are going to have to be very careful with your toys from now on. Jet is only a baby and so he doesn't know that these are your things and not to chew them.'

'Yes, Dad's right, we have got some toys for Jet, but from now on, don't leave around anything you don't want ruined.'

'We won't,' Tom and Jack said.

'By the way, Jack, here's Blue's present?' Mum said handing him a small wrapped parcel.

Jack tore the paper from the parcel to see Mum had knitted Blue his very own little black and tan dog.

'Look, Blue, you've got your very own dog. We'll have to think of a name for him,' Jack said, putting the dog beside Blue.

'What about LJ?' Dad said.

Jack was confused, until Dad explained.

'LJ for Little Jet,' he said looking at the dog beside Blue,

'And big Jet?' he said pointing to the puppy on the floor.

They all smiled and Jack said, 'I think it's a great name for your dog, Blue.'

Blue did too, as he looked at LJ and sincerely hoped that he wouldn't chew him like Jet had. He turned and looked again at Rose as she gave him a cheeky wink and smile.

12
BLUE'S FOOTBALL ADVENTURE

Jack and Taz were happily talking away as they came out of school. Jack had his rucksack on his back, and Blue's head was poking out of it, listening to their eager chatter.

'What's got you two so excited?' Mum said laughing, as she looked at Taz's Nan, Deliwe. Jet was jumping up and down happy to see the boys.

'Well, Mr Jones asked Taz if he wanted to join the seven aside football team which is brilliant. Oh, hello, Jet,' Jack said bending down and patting the dog on his head.

'That's great news, Taz,' his Nan said.

'Yes, well done, Taz. But, I thought all the teams were sorted already?' Mum replied.

'They were, but some of the boys and girls don't want to play anymore,' Jack said.

'But why? That's a real shame,' Mum said.

'I don't know,' Jack said shrugging his shoulders and shaking his head.

Mum said, 'I bet it's because they don't like playing outside when it's chilly. I hope you won't mind playing when the weather gets so cold, Taz?'

'No, I shall be fine,' Taz replied, beaming at her.

'I've told Taz that the team train every Wednesday after school, and that there's normally a match once a week,' Jack said, 'We've still got a few matches to play. And now that you're on the team, we won't lose our place in the tournament, because we've been playing really well, against the other schools on the island,' Jack said looking at Taz and smiling.

'I know, Blue and I have been standing there on the side lines shouting and encouraging you and Tom every time you've played.' Mum smiled at him.

With that Jack turned back and looked at Tom and said, 'Did you tell Mum that you're not going to play anymore?'

'Why, Tom?' Mum asked.

Tom just shrugged his shoulders.

'But I thought you liked playing with your brother and all your friends from the school?'

Tom shook his head. At every football match, Blue had been taken along to watch. That was where he had seen just how badly Tom played. Blue could see Tom's sad face, and he felt really sorry for him. Mr Jones liked to give everyone a chance at playing and Blue would always see the look of relief on Tom's face when he was called off to swap with someone else.

Blue loved going to watch and cheer the team on, especially since he had been made honorary mascot for them. Mum had made him a football kit in the same colours as the team, with an orange shirt with blue stripes, and matching shorts to wear every time they played.

Mum looked at Tom's miserable face, 'Here, do you want to take Jet and walk him back?'

Tom brightened up as he took the lead from her, talking away to the little dog as they walked towards home.

When they got there, Jack asked, 'Can Taz come in for a while?'

Mum nodded, Taz's Granddad popped his head out of their door and Mum asked him to join them for a cup of tea.

'Here you go, Mum,' Jack said handing her a piece of paper from his backpack, as he took Blue out of it.

'What's this, oh; it's your weekly newsletter,' Mum said quickly scanning it. 'I see they want some more parents to get involved with helping the football team. You might be interested in this, Eden,' Mum said showing him the newsletter.

'Yes I can't see why not. It would be great to help out. I used to help with the local team back in Zimbabwe, and if I say so myself, that team was very good. And that was all down to me!'

At that Taz looked at Jack and smiled.

'It would be great if Dad could help too,' Jack said, as his Dad came in the back door.

'Great if I could help with what?' Dad asked.

Jack told him all about the football team and the fact that Taz was now going to play with them. He also let slip that Tom wasn't going to play anymore.

Dad looked over at Tom, who was sitting at the table having a drink.

'Is that right, Tom, why? I thought you liked playing football.'

'No, I don't like it anymore,' he said sadly.

'Why don't you? Talk to me,' Dad said pulling a chair out and sitting down beside Tom.

'I can't seem to keep the ball when I get tackled, and then last week when I was near enough to score a goal, I kicked the ball and missed, and everyone got cross with me.' His bottom lip wobbled and Dad put his arms around Tom's shoulders.

'Not everyone is good at football, but I've seen you play, and you put your heart and soul into it. Are you sure you want to give it up. Isn't there any other positions you can play instead?' Dad asked.

Tom shook his head. 'No, Mr Jones has had me play most positions, apart from being goalie.'

'Billy Matthews is our goalie, and he's really good at it. In all the matches we've played this season, there have only been two balls go past him and that was because he'd fallen over. Otherwise, they'd never have got past him,' Jack butted in.

'And, if I was put into goal, our team would lose all the time,' Tom said forlornly.

'How about I help you with your footballing? What do you say?' Eden said.

Tom slowly nodded.

'Well then, there's no time like the present. Why don't you and Jack go and get changed into some other clothes, and then we can all go outside and kick the ball around for a while,' Dad said.

Tom looked pleased as he and Jack rushed into their bedrooms to get changed.

'I'll go home and get changed too,' Taz said.

For the next forty minutes Dad and Eden tried to coach Tom on how to dribble and swerve with the ball, every time an opposing player tried to tackle him. Tom tried his best to keep hold of the ball, but it was no use. What made it worse was when Jet took the ball from him, growling at him when Tom went to get it back. Blue saw all of this, as Jack had taken him outside with them and had placed him on the bench to watch.

'I think that's enough for now,' Dad said giving the boys a weary smile.

Jack bent down picking up the ball with one hand, getting it off Jet easily. Then he went over to the bench and picked up Blue before going back indoors.

'How did you get on?' Mum and Deliwe asked Tom as he came in.

Tom miserably shrugged his shoulders and shook his head.

'You'll get there in the end,' Eden said patting Tom on his shoulder.

Tom gave him a look that said he wasn't so sure.

'I'm going to get some tea going, would you like to stay?' Mum asked Taz who looked over at his grandparents for approval. They nodded and got up ready to go home.

'Why don't you boys go into the lounge and watch some telly,' Mum said as they all trooped into the room with Jet following close behind.

'Mum, can we play a game on the Wii?' Jack called out as he put Blue down on the sofa.

'Yes, but only for a little while.'

Jack went over to the television and switched it on. He picked a game for the Wii, looking at Taz and Tom.

'What about soccer?'

Taz and Tom nodded as Jack put it into the Wii. 'Tom, why don't you play Taz?' Jack said handing his brother the controller.

Taz was a striker in the game and as it was the only position he'd never played, Tom decided to be the goal keeper. As Taz's player got the ball, he started running down the pitch, dodging all the other players and making his way towards the goal where Tom's player was waiting. Suddenly, Taz's player kicked the ball and it looked like it was going into the goal, but then Tom's goalie got in the way as he leapt to the side, stopping the ball completely.

'That was a terrific save, Tom. What made you go that

way? I thought you were going the other,' Taz said smiling at Tom's happy face.

'I don't know I just seemed to know that's what you were going to do with your player. Do you want to carry on playing?' Tom asked Taz who quickly nodded at him.

The boys played, and each time Taz or Jack tried to score a goal, Tom seemed to know exactly what his goalie was meant to do, and he stopped them from getting the ball into the net, time after time.

Soon Mum called them in to the kitchen for their tea. The boys walked in, with Jack holding Blue as he and Taz were chatting and laughing away with Tom.

'What's made you all so happy?' Mum asked.

'It's Tom,' Jack said.

'Tom!' Mum said looking strangely at the boys.

'Yes, he's fantastic at being a goalie on the soccer game we just played,' Jack said as Taz nodded in agreement.

'Perhaps you've found the position you should be playing in football.'

Tom shook his head. 'No, I don't think I could compete with Billy Matthews.'

Mum looked at him and nodded.

At training on Wednesday, Dad and Eden and some other parents went along to give their support. When they got home they found Mum had tea ready and waiting for them on the table. Dad was outside, picking the mud out of their football boots.

'We've all been picked for the team on Friday, Mum,' Jack said excitedly bouncing up and down in his chair.

'That's great news that you've been picked to play, Tom,' said Mum.

'They only picked me, because there wasn't anyone else, so I'm back on the team.'

'I'm sure that's not true. There must be some other children that are still on the bench waiting to be picked for the team,' Mum replied.

'There are, but they're not very good either! I'm the best of the bunch,' Tom replied solemnly as he picked up his knife and fork and started eating his tea.

Jack looked at Tom's face and he started to smile, 'Tom, do you want to tell Mum what Dad has said she will do for the football team?'

At that, Tom started laughing as he looked up at his mum.

'Oh yeah, Dad said you would wash the football kit for everyone for the rest of the season, as Mrs Jones's washing machine has broken down!'

'He did, did he?'

Just then, Dad walked into the room, and the boys started to giggle.

As the weeks went on, the team were playing really well, all apart from Tom. Blue saw that Tom was always pleased to be taken off, after playing for just a few minutes. Luckily, Godshill School won every match and soon, they were in the final.

At the last training day, Dad and Eden were helping out with Mr Jones who was coaching the children. Miss Turner was also helping them keep fit with some exercises, before they had a trial game.

'Okay, everyone, listen up?' Mr Jones said. 'Now we are in the finals and playing against Newport Town School on Friday. They are a tough team to beat as they've won the trophy three years in a row.'

All the children nodded and some started mumbling to each other.

'Quiet please. I think we need a strong team if we are going to stand a chance at beating them. So for the first twenty minutes of the game, these are the boys and girls I would like to play. Jack Foster, Taz Mwamuka, Molly Bucket, Charlotte and Adam King, Billy Matthews and...' Mr Jones looked down at the list he had in his hand. 'Tom Foster.'

All the children looked at Tom, as he glanced away from their gloomy faces. Blue saw how sad Tom really was. When Tom had been training, the ball kept getting taken from him; and no matter how hard he tried to tackle it back, he couldn't get it from his opponent.

'And for the second half of the match, we'll see how it goes, but I will probably keep most of the players, and see about replacing Tom with Harriet Back.'

At that, Blue saw some of the children smile with what he thought was relief. Blue felt very sad for Tom.

The following Friday was match day against Newport Town. The parents were doubling up and taking the children in their cars, and as Mum and Dad had the 4 x 4, Taz, Deliwe and Eden were going with them. When they got there, Jack picked up Blue as he got out of the car.

'Mum, can you look after Blue for me; we're going over to Mr Jones to see what positions he wants us to play?'

She nodded taking hold of Blue, as the three boys went and found Mr Jones.

'Hello, Mr Jones,' Jack said, 'We've come to find out if we're still playing in the positions you gave us the other day?'

'We might not be playing, because we've been let down by a linesman. If we can't find another one, then we won't be playing at all. You don't know anyone who can run the line?' he asked them.

Jack and Taz turned around and called their parents over.

'I don't mind doing it,' Eden said when Mr Jones explained.

'That's great,' Mr Jones smiled as the rest of the team came over to him.

'Right, everyone gather round. We're just going to go over who's playing for us for the first half.' Suddenly, Mr Jones looked at the children. 'Where's Billy Matthews, has anyone seen him?'

The children shrugged their shoulders and shook their heads. All of a sudden, they heard the beep of a car horn, as they all looked over to see Billy getting out of his mum's car.

Mr Jones saw him and smiled.

'Billy, be careful, it's slippery there,' Jack shouted to him as he started running over to where they were. Suddenly, he slid and fell over. Jack and Taz raced over to him. Billy's, Mum, reached him at the same time. 'My ankle, it really hurts.' He sobbed as his mum put her arms around him trying to console him.

Mr Jones reached them a few seconds later.

'Are you alright, Billy? You can still play, can't you?' Jack asked.

Mrs Matthews shook her head as she tried to get Billy on his feet.

'Oww, it really hurts, Mum,' Billy wailed to her.

'It's no good, Mr Jones; I'm going to have to take him home. Look, it's already starting to swell,' she said pointing at Billy's ankle.

Mr Jones glumly nodded as Mrs Matthews helped Billy back to her car.

'Do you think we'll still play?' Taz whispered to Jack.

'I don't know?' Jack said as they all walked back over to where the other children were.

'Okay, there's a slight change of plan. Harriet you'll have to play in goal.'

'But… I…I don't want to Mr Jones. I'll get hit by the ball,' she said looking at him, before she suddenly burst into tears.

Mr Jones looked shocked. 'There, there, don't cry Harriet, if you really don't want to be in goal, you don't have to be,' he said scratching his head.

Tom spoke. 'What about me, Mr Jones? Could I try out as goalie? I've tried all the other positions and I wasn't very good,' he said shaking his head, 'but somehow I think I might be a good goalie. It's just something been telling me that that's the position I should play.'

Mr Jones nodded and suddenly smiled at Tom. 'Thank you for volunteering Tom, can you change out of your kit and slip on the green shirt and white shorts. I know you will give it your all.' Mr Jones smiled at him before he turned to Harriet and said, 'Will you play as one of our strikers then?'

At that Harriet nodded enthusiastically, before she turned to Tom, 'Thanks, Tom. I really didn't want to be in goal. I've seen how hard the ball flies at the goalie. Aren't you scared?'

Tom shook his head and said, 'No, I'm not. It's funny, but I had a dream where I was told I would be able to do this. And do you know what?' Harriet shook her head, 'I really think I can.'

Jack went up to Tom and gave him a playful punch on the arm as Tom smiled at him. They heard Mr Jones telling everyone to hurry up and change, before calling them all on to the pitch.

'Good luck everyone, remember what you've been taught. I know you'll all play your very best,' he said as he walked off the pitch and went and stood on the side with all the parents and supporters.

The referee threw a coin, and Jack who was captain called heads. It was tails, which meant the other side got the first kick of the ball. The two teams were playing really well as neither of them were letting the other team keep hold of the ball. Each time someone from Newport Town got the ball someone from Godshill School would retrieve it and force the ball back up the pitch again. However, before long one of the defenders from Newport Town was hurtling down towards the goal post where Tom was standing.

'Watch out, Tom,' Jack shouted as the ball was right near the goal post.

The striker took aim and fired, but Tom was ready for him. The ball looked like it was going in, until Tom threw himself on top of it, stopping it.

The crowd went wild; Mum with Blue in her arms was jumping up and down and shouting excitedly. 'Well done, Tom that was fantastic.' Then the referee blew his whistle, it was half time. The team trooped off the pitch and Mum and Deliwe were waiting for them with some squash and oranges slices. Taz was shivering, his teeth were chattering.

'Are you alright, Taz?' Mum asked.

'It's so… cold,' Taz said blowing on his hands trying to get them warm as Mum laughed at him.

'I thought you told me you would be fine playing in this weather,' she said as he smiled at her.

Mr Jones came up to them. 'Well done, you're all

playing brilliantly, especially you Tom.'

Everyone turned to Tom and smiled at him. 'Yes, you carry on playing like that, and we'll beat Newport Town no worries,' Harriet said.

The referee blew his whistle to let both teams know they were wanted back on the pitch. Mr Jones asked Charlotte and Adam to sit on the bench so that Valerie Jones and Anouska Penn could play for a while. The game started again, and both teams were playing well, until Valerie instead of kicking the ball, ended up kicking her opponent. The referee blew his whistle and decided to give Newport Town a free kick. Everyone on the team held their breath, as the opposing striker took his place in front of Tom who stood there waiting for him to kick the ball.

'Come on, Tom, you can do it. Don't let him get the ball in,' Mum shouted, gripping hold of Blue tightly.

The referee blew his whistle and the striker kicked the ball. It was as though the ball was being played in slow motion, as it curled towards the back of the net, when all of a sudden; Tom threw himself up and to the left hand side. Just in time he grabbed hold of the ball stopping it. The crowd went wild, screaming and shouting and Jack couldn't believe it when he looked over towards his parents seeing them jumping up and down hugging each other with Blue being jostled between them.

The full time whistle was blown and both coaches walked onto the pitch. After talking with the referee for a few minutes, they turned around and walked back to where the supporters were.

'We're playing extra time, another ten minutes,' Mr Jones said looking at the crowd as Blue in Mum's arms prayed Godshill School would score a goal.

'Come on guys you can do it,' Mum shouted to the team as they ran back to their places, before the referee blew his whistle to start extra time.

It was a nail biting five minutes, with Newport Town getting the ball down the field and near Tom a couple of times, but each time he was able to defend and prevent the ball from getting into the net. When five minutes were up, the teams swapped ends and the whistle was blown again for play to begin.

Jack had the ball and passed it to Taz, who kicked it to Molly. She was dribbling the ball down towards Newport Town's goalie, when she suddenly kicked it hard towards the goal. The ball went one way, and the goalie went the other. Everyone held their breath and Blue crossed his paws, praying the ball would go into the net, but it hit the side of the goal post and bounced off.

The final whistle went. The score was nil nil. There was nothing for it, there would have to be a penalty shoot-out. It would be the best out of five. The referee threw a coin again to decide who would go first. Godshill School won the toss. Jack was up and he positioned the ball in front of the goal. The goalie kept moving from side to side, as Jack took a couple of steps back and then ran at the ball. He kicked it and amazingly the ball went into the back of the net. The crowd went wild, cheering and yelling.

'Fantastic, Jack, yippee,' Mum called as Jack smiled and waved at her and Blue.

Then it was Tom's turn to be in goal. He watched the player from Newport Town as he stood in front of the ball. Jack looked at Tom. He seemed to know the ball was going to veer to the right. Suddenly, he saw Tom jump as the ball went towards him; he was ready to catch the ball and stop it from going in the net. Again, the crowd went mad.

'That's my boy, well done, Tom,' Mum screamed. Blue was so happy for Tom.

Taz was the next player from Godshill. He kicked the ball, but the goalie, managed to save it. This time there were moans and groans from the crowd. Then it was Tom up again. He got ready as the next striker took aim and kicked the ball. Once again, Tom managed to save the ball.

The next couple of balls played missed the goal too. It was almost over; Godshill School had one final kick. Harriet stood in front of the ball, she gave it one almighty strike and the ball flew into the back of the net. Godshill School had won the tournament.

Both teams congratulated one another, but Tom was the one getting all the fuss.

'You were fantastic, Tom. The way you saved those balls from going in, it was great,' Jack said.

'I couldn't agree more,' Dad said coming and gently squeezing Tom on the shoulder.

A couple of weeks later there was a presentation at Godshill School for their players. Two of them were going to receive special medals. There was one for player of the season, which was the team's choice; another was awarded most improved player by the parents.

'First, I would like to award the special medals to two of our team members,' Mr Jones said, 'It gives me great pleasure to present this medal for the player of the season to...'

The room went quiet.

'And this medal goes to... Billy Matthews.'

Billy stood up and hobbled to the front of the hall where he collected his medal. Everyone clapped him.

'The next medal goes to the most improved player of the season.'

Again everyone stopped talking.

'And it is with great honour I present this medal to… Tom Foster.'

At that Mum, Dad and Jack, who was holding Blue, were on their feet, clapping and cheering.

'Well done, Tom, that's great,' Harriet said as he walked past her to collect it.

'We have one final medal to give out. This year we decided to have a new medal for our mascot, Blue bear who looked excellent in his kit,' Mr Jones said as Jack eagerly took Blue up to collect his medal, shaking Blue's paws with Mr Jones and making everyone laugh.

Finally it was time to present the trophy cup.

'And the winning team of the tournament, from our very own Godshill School, please come up and have your photograph taken with the trophy cup.'

Everyone clapped and cheered the team, and photos were taken for the local paper, The County Press, with Blue sitting right in the middle. Afterwards Mr Jones came up to Jack and his family.

'Well done boys, you both played brilliantly. I can't wait for next season to come round again,' Mr Jones said, 'And, I think Tom will be sharing the position of goalie with Billy.' Then Mr Jones turned to Mum, 'Mrs Foster, I understand that you've said you don't mind carrying on washing the kit for us.'

At that, Mum glared at Dad, while Jack and Tom giggled at each other.

Jack cuddled Blue and said, 'You really were our lucky mascot, I can't wait for next season now.'

13
BLUE'S SCHOOL FETE ADVENTURE

Jack came rushing out of school, holding Blue in his arms. He looked really excited, as he hurried over to Mum and Tom waving the school's newsletter at them.

'Tom, have you told Mum the news that the school's going to have a fete?'

Tom shook his head as Jack turned towards her.

'Mum, they are going to have a fete and they want parents to volunteer to help. I told Mrs Ansell that you would lend them a hand helping out,' Jack said smiling at her.

Mum's face fell.

'Oh, Jack, I really don't know if I can. It all depends what day the fete's on,' Mum shook her head. 'If it's on during the week, then there's no way I can help. You know how busy I get at the surgery.'

Jack beamed. 'It's alright, Mum, the fete's going to be on the last Saturday in June. That's why I told Mrs Ansell you could help. In the newsletter, they are asking parents to lend a hand with stalls and organizing setting up on the day.'

Mum nodded. 'Alright, Jack, if you wait here with Tom, I'll just pop in and have a word with Mrs Ansell.

As Mum walked away Jack looked at the newsletter.

'Mrs Ansell said there will be a tombola stall; guess the weight of the sweets, a raffle stall and lots of other stalls. Did you know they're even having a dog show?'

Tom said, 'We might be able to enter Jet in it.'

Jack nodded. 'He might even get a prize!'

At that Tom raised his eyebrows and laughed.
'What for being the naughtiest dog there?'

Jack giggled.

'Anyway, it's going to be great fun, and this year we'll be having it up on the cricket field. Mrs Ansell said it was so they could fit more stalls in, so it will be amazing,' Jack said still cuddling Blue as Mum came back out towards them.

Mum was smiling as she reached them.

'That's all sorted, I've told Mrs Ansell I'll be available to help out on the day, and she's going to arrange with the PTA to get in touch with me. But, that's not the only good news, because I've put yours and Tom's names down to do… country dancing with the girls!'

'What! No way,' both boys cried out.

Blue looked at Jack wondering why he didn't want to do the dancing.

'I don't want to do any dancing, only sissys do dancing,' Tom said looking disgusted, 'especially with the girls, yuck!'

Jack's face said it all too.

'Mum, you'll have to tell Mrs Ansell we can't do it, as we don't know how to dance.'

Mum smiled and said, 'Oh, that's alright, don't you worry about that. After school on a Wednesday and a Friday afternoon, from 3pm to 4pm, that's when Mrs Cole will be putting you though your dance routines. You will be practicing the dances, and will know them very well before the big day.'

'But, Mum…' Jack wailed.

'No, buts, if I'm doing something to help with the fete, then so are you, and that's all there is to it,' Mum said firmly.

Both boys pulled faces, and Blue gave a small smile as he looked at them. Perhaps dancing wouldn't be so bad after all, it might even be fun.

In the coming weeks, before the fete, the boys went each Wednesday and Friday after school to practice their country dancing. The first time they went Jack put his rucksack with Blue in it on top of the benches, so Blue had a bird's eye view of the children as they learnt their moves.

Mrs Cole was in charge. She started pairing up the boys and girls.

'Jack, I would like you and Molly to pair up, and Tom, can you pair up with Nancy Ward, please?'

The boys walked reluctantly over to their partners.

'Right, everyone, if you can form a circle, I will explain exactly what I want you to do,' Mrs Cole said.

The children quickly got into a circle and Mrs Cole asked them to sit down.

'I'm going to play the music for you first, so that you know what you will be dancing to,' with that she went over and pushed the button for the music to start.

From where he was sitting, Blue could hear the music and he liked it. His paws were moving with the beat of the tune. As soon as the music finished, Mrs Cole switched it off.

'Watch while I show you what steps I want you to do. I'll need a partner,' she looked around the circle and made her way over to Jack.

'Will you be my partner, Jack?'

Jack nodded feeling his face grow warm as he stumbled to his feet, he felt embarrassed, especially when he had to hold hands with Mrs Cole. Tom started giggling at him, but soon stopped when Jack looked over at him and glared

'Right, Jack, we will skip together, going round in a circle, once we have gone one way, we will turn and go the other.'

They did that, and then stopped. 'We will need another couple of volunteers, Tom and Nancy can you come over here, please?'

Nancy instantly shot to her feet, but Tom wasn't so keen, and sighed heavily as he got up. When they got to Mrs Cole, Jack started sniggering.

'That's enough of that please, Jack,' Mrs Cole said. 'Now, Tom and Nancy, if you face us, I will show you what I want you to do. It's very simple, we are going to move towards one another and back again, and then the opposite partner is going to swap places. We are going to do a doe-see-doe step, once, then we are going to do it again, but this time we will stay with that partner. So I will be with Tom and you, Nancy, will be with Jack. Afterwards, we will do the first step again of going around in a circle one way, and then back the opposite direction. Has everyone got that?'

Everyone sitting on the floor watching nodded their heads.

'We will do this once, to show you, and then I want everyone to join in.'

Mrs Cole went back to the music and turned it on again.

'I'll count us in, one…two…three…and begin.'

Blue loved the country dancing; his paws were constantly tapping away with the music. He couldn't wait to go home and tell Rose all about it. He was sure she would love to see the children dancing too, but that might be difficult, as she was always kept out of the way, on top of Mum's chest of drawers. Mum had said she was not a toy for playing with, but perhaps there could be a way of her seeing them.

The day of the fete dawned bright and sunny and in Jack's house everyone was up early. Mum had volunteered Dad to help out too. Everyone had kept their fingers crossed that the sun would shine, so it was a relief when the weather forecaster said there would be sunshine with the slight chance of rain later in the day.

'If it rains, will we have to cancel our country dancing?' Jack asked ever hopeful looking at Tom with crossed fingers.

'No, if it looks like it's going to rain, then Mrs Cole has arranged that the country dancing will take place inside one of the marquees,' Mum said smiling at the boys as the look of hope faded from Jack and Tom's faces.

'Have you boys got everything, because once we go today, we won't be coming home until after the fete is over.'

Jack reluctantly walked back to his bedroom to collect his rucksack. Blue was sitting on the breakfast bar waiting for him to come back.

'Here you go Blue,' Jack said trying to squeeze Blue into his bag.

However, Blue wouldn't seem to fit in.

'Why won't you go in?' Jack asked, putting Blue back on the breakfast bar.

Just as Jack was about to empty his bag, Mum called out they were going. So picking Blue up, Jack put him under his arm, and chucked his bag over his shoulder and headed outside to the others.

When they got to the playing field, everyone was busy

sorting out all the stalls. Dad was helping some of the other parents put up the marquee and Mum was helping out with the refreshment stall. Jack went round helping out where he could, and Tom was walking Jet round the field keeping him out of trouble. Jack had put Blue down on the floor beside his rucksack, where Mum was busy setting up the cakes to sell.

No one was looking at Blue as he stood up and pulled the rucksack open.

'Are you alright?' he whispered to…Rose.

'Yes, I'm fine, don't worry about me. It's so exciting to finally be outside for once,' she smiled up at him.

'Hopefully, we won't have too long to wait until the fete opens and then straight away; the children will be doing their dancing. You will know when it's going to start, because of the music playing,' Blue said smiling down at her.

'This is such a wonderful adventure for me, Blue. Thank you for thinking about how I could come and see it,' Rose giggled.

Soon there were crowds of people waiting and before long, it was time for the High Sherriff to announce the fete was officially open. Straight after that it was time for the children to kick off the proceedings with their country dancing. Blue whispered to Rose, 'it's time,' then she carefully pulled herself to the top of the rucksack, peeping out.

Mrs Cole pressed play and music filled the arena as the children walked in a circle to begin their dancing.

'Blue, you are right, this music is very catchy,' Rose said clapping her paws together.

The music drew to an end and the audience all clapped as the children stopped and took a bow. Someone shouted out, 'more' and Mrs Cole switched the music back on again and the children did another dance.

'This is wonderful; I'm so pleased I could see it? It was a great idea of yours to smuggle me out in Jack's rucksack.' Rose smiled.

'I know, and hopefully with Mum being busy, she will be tired at the end of the day and so we will be able to get you back on top of the chest of drawers, without her knowing that you have been anywhere,' Blue replied, winking at her.

The day passed by very quickly, and before long it was time to go home. It was just as Blue thought; everyone was very tired, but happy. Jet had even won a rosette at the dog show, for having the waggiest of tails. Mum had won a bottle of wine on the raffle, and Jack and Tom had been lucky with the tombola winning some sweets. They all stayed behind to help pack everything away, and Blue was picked up by Mum, along with the rucksack when they were ready to go home. Rose hid at the bottom of it, hoping Mum wouldn't open it up, and, fortunately she didn't.

When they got home, Jack took Blue and his rucksack into his bedroom.

'I hope you've had a good day today Blue, and that you enjoyed my country dancing?' Jack said giving his pal a cuddle.

What Jack didn't see was Blue giving Rose a sly wink as she nodded her head at him, before she eased herself out of the rucksack and quietly and quickly made her way back to Mum and Dad's bedroom.

14
BLUE'S DOG TRAINING ADVENTURE

One Friday afternoon, Mum was standing waiting at the school gates with Tom when Jack, came rushing out into the playground with his friends.

'Bye, see you Tuesday?' Jack shouted waving to Adam and Charlotte as they hurried over to their Dad's car before he ran over to Mum.

'Jack, what do you mean you'll see the twins on Tuesday, surely, you mean Monday?' Mum said looking quizzically at him.

Jack shook his head. 'No, that's right. Monday we have the day off, as it's a teacher training day,' he said as he adjusted his rucksack, pulling Blue out of the back of it and holding him in his arms.

'Blow it, I forgot all about that. Perhaps Sam Farren can look after you and Tom, as I've got to work all day at the surgery,' Mum muttered.

'Mum, you've forgotten, Sam's gone away on holiday? We saw her in the Post Office, and she said she was going away for two weeks?' Tom piped up.

Mum winced as she nodded. 'Yes, of course, I did forget. And, there's no way I can get the day off, as we've got staff on holiday too. I wonder if you'll be able to go to work with Dad, on Monday instead,' she said looking at the boys as they began walking home.

Jack looked at Blue and said, 'I think we're going to be bored on Monday!'

Blue really hoped they wouldn't be.

When they got home, Dad was in the back garden with Jet who was running round and round in circles, barking madly.

'Good boy, Jet,' Jack called as he rushed over to him and Tom and they bent down to make a fuss of him.

'Have you had a good day, Dad?' Tom asked.

'No, not really, Jet's been a bit of a pain.'

'Why, what did he do?' Jack asked looking at the excited puppy and tickling his tummy.

'Well I've been doing some gardening work for Mrs Russell and every time I planted some new shrubs, a few minutes later, Jet would come along and dig them up.'

Jack and Tom both burst out laughing, but immediately stopped when they saw the stern look on Dad's face.

'It wasn't funny. I put a lot of hard work in today and it was all for nothing. It was a good job, Mrs Russell wasn't around,' he said shaking his head and looking quite cross with Jet.

Blue looked at Jet and was glad that his own dog, LJ was a good little dog. Often when Jack was fast asleep at night, Blue would teach LJ some of the things he'd seen Mum trying to get Jet to do. Although, Jet wasn't that good at doing as he was told, LJ was. Recently, Mum had spoken about taking Jet to dog training classes, but nothing had come of it.

'Did you try telling him to sit and stay?' Jack asked as Dad nodded.

'I did, and he did as he was told for a while, but then because I wasn't paying any attention to him, he started playing up.'

'Well, if that's the case, then I've got some good news for you?' Mum said smiling at Dad and winking at the boys.

The following Monday morning, before Mum went to work she gave the boys some food to take with them.

'I've made you some sandwiches and put some fruit in. Dad's got a flask of coffee, and there are some cartons of orange juice for you boys. In the rucksack, I've put in a couple of Jet's doggy chews for him too,' Mum said handing the rucksack to Tom.

'I'm off to work now, so I'll see you all when you come home,' she said giving the boys a kiss as they got ready to go with Dad to Mrs Russell's house.

'Now boys, I can trust you to keep an eye on Jet and make sure he doesn't get up to any mischief whilst I'm busy gardening, can't I?' Dad asked.

'Yes, Dad, we'll play with him and keep him out of your way. Blue has even brought LJ along, haven't you?' Jack looked as his pal sat in the back of his rucksack as Blue had his paws firmly around his little dog.

'Come on then, I don't want to keep Mrs Russell waiting as I've still got quite a bit to do there.'

The boys got in Dad's work van and strapped themselves in. Jack took Blue out of his rucksack, but no sooner had he put him on his lap than Jet grabbed hold of Blue's leg.

'No, Jet let go of Blue,' Jack said trying to get the dog's teeth away from his pal.

Tom had to hold Jet and gently prise his mouth open for him to let go in the end.

'Perhaps you'd better keep Blue out of Jet's way for the time being,' Dad said looking at the boys in his rear view mirror as they sat in the back of the van. Jack nodded putting Blue back in his rucksack again.

But things didn't improve once they got to Mrs

Russell's house. The moment the boys opened the van door, Jet jumped out and started running all over the garden.

'Bad dog, Jet,' Dad shouted at him as he started chasing Jet trying to get hold of him.

Tom and Jack joined in running round the garden trying to get hold of the little dog, but Jet thought it was a game and just barked at them whenever they got close enough to grab him and then ran off again. It was only when Mrs Russell opened her front door and Jet was close enough to her that she was able to bend down and pick him up.

Jet was wriggling in her arms, but she held him firm and refused to let him go.

'Have you got his lead?' she asked Tom, who rushed to the van and picked it up taking it across to her as she clicked the clasp onto his collar.

Placing Jet down on the ground she looked at him and with her hand on his bottom pushing him down, she said, 'Sit.'

Jet surprised everyone by doing as he was told.

'I'm so sorry, Mrs Russell, he just gets so excited, especially as I've had to bring my boys with me today. Their school is having a teacher training day, but, I promise you, they won't make any noise and they'll keep Jet in line,' Dad said looking slightly worried as he looked at the expression on her face.

Suddenly, Mrs Russell smiled. 'What have I told you, call me Isobel, and it's fine you brought your sons and your dog with you today. I love dogs, I always have. We've always had them,' she said smiling at the boys as she looked back down at Jet who was still sitting patiently by her side.

'I can't believe Jet's still sitting there,' Tom said looking at the dog as he stayed put.

'Look, why don't you get on and the boys and Jet can come indoors for a while,' Isobel said talking gently to Jet, as she guided him inside. 'Heal, good boy,' she said walking towards the kitchen as the boys who had grabbed their rucksacks followed behind her.

'Could you close the door, then I will take Jet's lead off?'

Tom shut the door, and Isobel unclasped the lead, as Tom and Jack stood there.

'Sit down, boys,' Isobel said indicating to her kitchen table.

Jack took Blue out of his rucksack and sat him down on the table, putting LJ beside him.

'That's lovely,' Isobel said picking LJ up. 'Is he a good boy for you?' she asked Blue as she looked at Jack and winked.

'Well LJ's is a lot better behaved than Jet,' Jack said looking at the dog as all of a sudden, he started jumping up at Isobel.

'Jet, off,' Isobel said with a firm tone. Jet once again surprised the boys by doing as he was told. 'Good boy, sit,' Isobel said all the while keeping eye contact with Jet, who sat obediently at Isobel's feet.

'Jet's being so good for you?' Tom said.

'Well, it's all down to how you train your dog, being firm, but fair with them. They have to know there are rules and that they have to follow them.'

'Well we were going to take Jet to puppy training classes, but Mum hasn't found one yet, and so we have been trying to train him, but we've not been doing very well,' Jack said shaking his head.

'That's the trouble, when you take a dog on, you have to find the time to do some training, even the most basic of training, because in the end it is what will make all the difference between having a good dog and a bad dog. I've had lots of experience in training dogs. I've run training schools in the past, so perhaps I can help you boys teach Jet a couple of commands?'

Tom and Jack nodded as Blue listened, keen to know what other training Jet could be taught, and whether he could teach it to LJ too.

'The most important thing is the recall. When you're all at home, getting Jet to come back when he's called is the key to success.'

Again Tom and Jack nodded.

'Once they come to their name, give them praise and at the beginning reward them. This can be with a toy or treat or just a big fuss!'

At that the boys looked at one another and smiled.

'Jet loves his squeaky toys, especially his toy bone and is always playing with it. That's until Mum or Dad take it off him as he keeps on squeaking and being noisy with it,' Jack said laughing as he told her how the dog had sulked when he could no longer play with it the night before.

'We have a couple of Jet's treats here,' Tom said opening up the rucksack and handing them over to Isobel.

'That's great, but I think I have something Jet will love a bit more, and respond better to,' she said walking over to her fridge.

Isobel brought out a plate that had some pieces of meat on it.

'This was left over from my tea last night, and I was going to have a cold meat sandwich, but I think we can use it as a reward when Jet does the right thing instead,' she said smiling at the boys as she cut the meat into small pieces. 'Shall we take Jet out into the back garden and see how we get on?' Isobel said picking up an old ball from her unit and putting it in her pocket.

At that the boys stood up and Jack picked up Blue from the table as Isobel opened the back door. Jet immediately ran off, and the boys went to run after him, but Isobel stopped them.

'Wait boys. Here, Jet, come here,' she called to him.

All of a sudden, he stopped running and looked over at her.

'Come here, Jet, good boy,' she said bending down and encouraging him back over to her.

Slowly, Jet made his way back to her as Isobel held out her hand to show him the treat she had for him. Jet went to grab the treat and as he did, Isobel held onto his collar, making a fuss of him and telling him what a good boy he was.

'Do you boys want to have a go?'

'Yes, please.'

With that Isobel let go of Jet's collar and took the ball from her pocket and threw it for him. As soon as Jet saw the ball, he ran after it, stopping and grabbing it in his mouth.

'Tom, do you want to try calling Jet back?' Isobel said as she handed him some of the meat.

Tom started calling Jet, but he paid no attention to him. Jet was happy playing with his ball.

'Look, why don't you bend down and put the treat on your hand, showing it to him?' Isobel suggested.

Tom did as he was told, still calling to Jet. Suddenly, Jet seemed to sniff the air as he turned back around towards Tom. He dropped the ball and raced over towards him. When he got there, as soon as he spied the treat on Tom's hand he bent his head to gobble it up. Tom quickly grabbed hold of Jet's collar, all the while praising him.

'Good boy, well done.'

'Tom, that was fantastic,' Jack said smiling at him. Blue was also impressed and couldn't wait to try that with LJ.

Isobel walked over to Tom and put the lead back on Jet.

'Now we are going to try another command, which is sit. I want you to watch me as I walk with Jet. I think it is very important, when you come to a road that you always make your dog sit before you cross.'

With that Isobel started walking with Jet telling him to heel. She had a piece of a treat in her hand and Jet could smell it as he kept pace with her as she walked around the garden.

Abruptly, she said, 'Sit,' and placing her hand on Jet's bottom, she gently pushed him down, into a sitting position. All the while she was praising him by telling him what a good boy he was.

'Jack, do you want to come over here and take over from me?'

With that, Jack handed Blue to Tom to hold while he went over to take the lead from Isobel.

'Just do what I did, here have the treat in your hand and let Jet sniff your hand to know it's there.'

Jack started walking, calling Jet to heel as he moved around the garden. When he felt it was the right time, he told Jet to sit, gently pushing down on Jet's bottom. With that the dog once again did as he was told.

'Good boy, Jet,' Jack said giving the dog his treat and making a real fuss of him.

'Wow, that was great,' Dad said coming up to Jack and bending down he patted Jet on his head.

Tom and Isobel came over to them.

'Isobel has been teaching us a few easy commands,' Tom said.

'Yes, and if you keep it up, I can't see why Jet won't keep on doing them. All it takes is patience and time, just five minutes every day. Repeat it all the time and Jet will get it,' she said bending down and stroking his ears.

'I heard you out here and I was worried Jet was playing up, so came to find you?' Dad said.

'No, we're all fine as you can see?' Isobel smiled as she walked over to Jack. 'Here, take this bit of treat and hold it in your hand.'

Jack took it from her.

'Shall we try letting Jet off his lead and see how he behaves when we walk round to the front garden?' Isobel said.

Jack looked over at his Dad and saw his face fall. As Jack bent down to take the lead off Jet he began talking to him and showing him the treat in his hand. Jack slowly started walking towards the front garden and Jet was walking to heel following by his side sniffing the treat in his hand.

'You are such a good boy,' Jack said as he told Jet to sit when they got there.

This time he didn't have to put his hand on Jet's bottom, as Jet automatically sat when Jack told him to. Giving him his treat as Isobel came up to them, Jack then put the lead back on.

'Well done you. If you and Tom do that every day with Jet, it won't take long to get him trained. And, you'll be able to show your Mum and Dad what to do with Jet too.'

'That would be great,' Dad said. 'He isn't a bad dog; we've just got to find the time to train him. You're right there; Isobel, all it takes is patience and time.'

'The garden's coming on a treat. Why don't you and the boys come back into the kitchen and have a drink. Looking at Jet, I think he's had enough training for the moment. What do you say?' Isobel said smiling at them all.

'That would be great,' Dad said taking the lead from Jack and encouraging Jet to walk to heel as they went back to the kitchen door.

Blue was so pleased the boys had a teacher training day, as instead of it being a boring one, he had learnt so much watching as Jet was trained. Blue thought he couldn't wait to try it with LJ later. He did enjoy all the exciting adventures he had with Jack. He smiled at his little dog who was still sitting waiting patiently for him on the kitchen table.

ABOUT THE AUTHOR

Maggie Jones lives on the beautiful Isle of Wight, where she finds her inspiration to write her stories. Her genres are romance, comedy and drama. Bessie's Rescue was her first story published with Alfie Dog, she has since had further stories published, including stories in the compilations 'Came as Me, Left as We,', 'A Wish for Christmas', and 'Read it Again'. Maggie is chairperson of The Wight Fair Writers www.iowwritingcircle.co.uk and they hold two competitions every year. All revenue from these competitions goes to support local Charities.

She has a Facebook page The Wight Fair Writers' Circle facebook.com/groups/622709414412970/ where likeminded authors share tips and ideas.

Maggie Jones' stories also appear in

A Wish for Christmas – The Christmas Collection
Came as 'Me', Left as 'We' – Women's Fiction
Read it Again – Children's Collection

38052601R00088